The Vampire's Revenge

It was Lady Fossington-Twiste who was the first to move. As the full horror of the situation gradually dawned upon her, she got slowly to her feet, her face deathly pale.

"I danced with Dracula!" she wailed in a high-pitched voice which travelled all around the room, silencing the conversation at the other tables. It was sufficient to cause consternation among the musicians, bringing their dance music to a sudden stop. "I was partnered by a blood-drinking vampire!"

by the same author

The Last Vampire
Henry Hollins and the Dinosaur
The Inflatable Shop
Return of the *Antelope*
The *Antelope* Company Ashore
The Vampire's Holiday

THE
VAMPIRE'S
REVENGE

Willis Hall

Illustrated by Tony Ross

RED FOX

A Red Fox Book

Published by Random House Children's Books
20 Vauxhall Bridge Road, London SW1V 2SA

A division of Random House UK Ltd
London Melbourne Sydney Auckland
Johannesburg and agencies throughout the world

1 3 5 7 9 10 8 6 4 2

First published in Great Britain by The Bodley Head 1993

Red Fox edition 1994

Printed and bound in Great Britain by
Cox & Wyman Ltd, Reading, Berkshire

RANDOM HOUSE UK Limited Reg. No. 954009

ISBN 0 09 929881 3

The Vampire's Revenge

1

"Ouch!"

Count Alucard, the last surviving member in the long line of Transylvanian vampires, touched tentatively at his chin and then grimaced as he peered at the spot of blood on the tip of his forefinger. The Count shivered, but it had nothing to do with the temperature of the room. Count Alucard could not stand the sight of blood – particularly if it happened to be his own.

He stared, gloomily, into the cracked mirror above the tiny sink which was jammed into a corner of the room. But looking into the mirror served little purpose, for, as always, he was not rewarded with the sight of his own familiar features gazing back at him. Count Alucard, like all vampires, had no reflection when he looked into a looking-glass.

This made it very difficult for him to shave. He was constantly nicking himself with his razor, just as he had done a moment before. Combing his hair was another problem for, without ever being able to see himself in the mirror, it was difficult to make a neat parting. For that reason, the Count chose to comb his long black hair straight back over his head without any attempt at all at making a parting.

Count Alucard let out a long, sad sigh.

The Count was feeling rather sorry for himself that morning. Not just because he had cut himself while shaving; nor even because of the difficulty he had when trying to manipulate a comb. No, the truth of the matter was that there were times when Count Alucard wished that he was an ordinary human being. Although he was very proud of his family name, there were mornings when he woke up wishing that he hadn't been born a vampire.

This was one of those mornings.

Still gazing into the mirror, he could see the entire contents of his bedroom in the English country cottage where he was presently staying as a paying guest.

He could see the old-fashioned, enormous walnut wardrobe with its matching chest of drawers, on top of which there stood, on a crocheted doily, a small chipped vase containing a selection of wild flowers. He could see the framed picture of two kittens peeping out of a basket, hanging over the brass bedstead, and the pretty patchwork quilt spread neatly over the made-up bed.

The Count had not slept in the bed that previous night. He had chosen to sleep, as he always did, in the satin-lined, highly polished, black wooden coffin which was taking up most of the floor space in the little bedroom. Count Alucard had managed to smuggle in the coffin through the back door one night while old Mrs Prendergast, his landlady, had been out in the front garden calling in her cat.

The bedroom itself was pleasant enough, though rather cramped for space when compared to the

vast and sprawling Castle Alucard, where he had
grown up, with its spacious stone-walled rooms,
turreted roofs, vaulted ceilings and spiralling stone
staircases.

All of that had been lost to him on the night,
some years before, when the Transylvanian villagers, fearing the Dracula vampire legend, armed
with scythes and sticks and stones and some of them
bearing blazing torches, had stormed the castle and
burned it to the ground.

Count Alucard shuddered again as he recalled that
awful night on which he had been lucky to escape
with his life. But that had not been the only time
when the Castle Alucard had been destroyed. The
very same thing had happened when his father had
lived in the castle and, once before that, when his
grandfather had been in residence.

On three separate occasions, the Castle Alucard had been built high up on the mountainside and, on three separate occasions, the villagers had swarmed up from their homes below, with their scythes and sticks and stones and blazing torches, and destroyed the Alucard family seat.

All of which, the Count told himself, might arguably have been no more nor less than his father and his father before him had deserved – but as far as his own case was concerned it did seem a little unfair. For he had never ever, when all was said and done, sunk his pointy teeth into anyone.

Count Alucard pulled a distasteful face at the very idea of biting somebody on the neck – or, for that matter, on any other part of his or her anatomy. Unlike his forebears, the Count was not a vampire in the true sense of the word. Although he could, whenever he so desired, change himself into a bat – the bat that he turned into was a nervous, nose-twitching fruit-bat and not a blood-drinking monster.

For this last proud, remaining member of the Dracula clan was a dedicated vegetarian through and through.

"But just try telling that to a gang of villagers once they have got their danders up," the Count murmured softly to himself. "You've only got to mention the name Dracula to villagers – and I don't care which village it is they come from – and they'll be reaching for their blazing torches and their glistening scythes—"

"Mr Alucard?" Old Mrs Prendergast's precise voice broke in on his thoughts, calling to him through the door of his room and addressing him by the name that he had chosen to put in the *Visitor's Book* on the hall table when he had first arrived. To have announced himself as a Transylvanian Count would only have been asking for trouble. "Are you up and about?" continued the old lady, rapping on the door. "May I trouble you for a moment?"

"Just a second, Mrs Prendergast!" gulped the Count, pushing his memories to the back of his mind. "I shan't detain you very long!"

Then, crossing the room in two short strides, he stooped down, hoisted the long black coffin up onto one end and, balancing it on his shoulder, opened the wardrobe's double doors and manouevred it inside. Slamming the doors shut on the coffin, he turned, lifted down the patchwork counterpane and ruffled the sheets and pillow to make it look as if he had slept in the bed. Smoothing down his silk purple dressing-gown, Count Alucard flicked back his hair with thumbs and forefingers, sat down in the wicker-work chair close by the window and folded his hands, neatly, on his lap.

"Do come in, Mrs Prendergast!"

"Good morning, Mr Alucard," said that chubby and good-natured lady, as she entered the Count's bedroom and proferred him a large envelope. "This came for you in the post this morning."

"Thank you, dear lady," replied the Count, rising to his feet politely. His long pale fingers reached out to take the envelope which he had recognised instantly. It contained the latest issue of *The Coffin-Maker's Journal*, which he looked forward eagerly to reading every month.

"I was also wondering whether you might care for me to cook you a *proper* breakfast this morning?" As she spoke, Mrs Prendergast's eyes took in the room. She beamed approvingly at the apple-pie orderliness of the interior. Apart from the unmade bed, her lodger's quarters were as neat and tidy as the day on which she had last given it a thorough going-over with the vacuum cleaner, two yellow dusters and a tin of pine-scented furniture polish. The old lady appreciated having such a fastidious guest. She was more than willing to make his stay with her a happy one. She also thought him such a pale, thin gentleman that a change of diet might do him the world of good. "How about some nice pork sausages?" she suggested. "And some rashers of crispy bacon?"

"It's extremely kind of you to offer, dear lady," replied the Count with a firm shake of his head, "but my usual glass-of-orange-juice-and-half-a-grapefruit will be more than sufficient I assure you."

"Can't I even tempt you with a slice of buttered wholewheat toast?" The old lady sounded disappointed.

"Well, yes – all right then – just a single slice of toast," murmured the Count, edging his landlady towards the door.

Count Alucard was eager to have the room to himself again. He wanted to flick through the pages of *The Coffin-Maker's Journal* before breakfast. He was keen to scan the advertisements. He had been sleeping in the selfsame coffin (the one tucked out of sight in the wardrobe) for many a long year. Its padded base was getting lumpy. The satin headrest was soiled and showing signs of wear. It was about time, he had decided, to consider investing in a new coffin. Perhaps this latest issue of his favourite magazine might be advertising the sort of brand new model he was looking for . . . ?

As soon as the door had closed behind his land-lady, Count Alucard ripped open the buff envelope and drew out the glossy magazine contained within. Tossing the envelope aside, he sat down in the wickerwork chair and flicked through the colourful pages.

There was, he soon discovered, a beautiful new craftsman-constructed cabinet on the market. It was fashioned from the very best mahogany and had the finest polished brass hinges, fixtures and fittings. Exactly the kind of thing he had been looking for! He might just spread his bat's wings the next fine moonlit evening and fly down to the nearest funeral director's parlour. He would ask permission to stretch out in one of the new coffins for half an hour, just to try it out for size and comfort. Life, he decided, was well worth the living!

Feeling chirpier by the second, Count Alucard put down his magazine, took off his dressing-gown and began to put on his clothes.

Even without the benefit of a mirror, the Count was able to dress neatly and quickly. It was all a matter of habit. For, no matter what the occasion, the Count always wore the same clothes: black suit, starched white shirt with wing collar, black bow tie and a gold medallion suspended on a gold chain around his neck. If going out of doors, the Count added a scarlet-lined black cloak to his ensemble.

Count Alucard whistled to himself, cheerfully, as he knotted his black bow tie. The downcast mood of minutes before had gone completely. The possibility of a comfortable new coffin had quite cheered him up.

He was looking forward to breakfast too. Mrs Prendergast always saw to it, when doing her weekly shopping, that she chose the juiciest of grapefruits for her lodger. The orange juice, too, that she presented him with each morning, was freshly squeezed out of fruit which she had personally selected from off the greengrocer's shelves.

The vegetarian vampire Count licked his lips in anticipation at the fruity meal ahead. He ran his tongue over his pointy teeth and smiled as he considered how foolish he had been in feeling downhearted. Just what had he got to complain about, he asked himself? Admittedly, his room was small – but it was cosy enough and comfortable.

Glancing out of the window, and looking down into Mrs Prendergast's cottage garden, he enjoyed the whole blaze of colour provided by the hollyhocks, hydrangeas and the honeysuckle all in full blossom in the early morning midsummer sunlight. The Count's spirits rose even higher. Not only was there no cause for him to feel down in the mouth – on the contrary, he had every reason to rejoice at simply being alive!

Count Alucard leaned out of the window and sniffed deeply at the rich scent of flowers rising up on the warm air. It was at this precise moment, just as he was considering his blessings, that the Count chanced to glance beyond the garden and what he glimpsed caused his heart to sink immediately into his black patent leather pointed shoes.

Striding out towards the cottage, along the lane that led from the village, was a group of angry villagers. Although they were still some way away, the Count could see that some of them were carrying scythes, while others wielded sticks and several brandished blazing torches.

"Oh, my word!" said Count Alucard glumly to himself. "I fear that history is about to repeat itself! But how did they know that I was staying in the district?"

Turning back into the room, the Count stooped and picked up the buff coloured envelope which had recently contained his *Coffin-Maker's Journal*. He noted that the envelope was addressed to "The Count Alucard" and, also, that it bore a Transylvanian postmark.

Glancing out of the window once again, he saw that the group of villagers was drawing closer. He could hear the angry murmur of their voices on the breeze. Among their numbers, he could now make out the milkman, the shopkeeper, the man who kept the village pub and – yes – the postman.

Putting two and two together, Count Alucard had little difficulty in guessing who had discovered that a member of the Dracula family was living close by the village.

Even with her failing eyesight, Mrs Prendergast might just have noticed the noble title and the give-away postmark on the envelope – but even if she had spotted them, the Count told himself, she would hardly have announced his presence to the entire village without so much as having a word with him first. No, she was much too honest and kind a person for such behaviour. The postman, on the other hand, was an altogether different proposition. The Count had observed the fellow, only the other afternoon, peering at him inquisitively from behind the cottage garden's water barrel . . .

But this was hardly the time and place for guessing games. Several of the approaching villagers, he saw, were carrying placards and they were now close enough for him to read the hastily painted words.

There was not a moment to be lost. Within seconds, the villagers, now buzzing like a storm of angry hornets, would be coming up the cottage's garden path. Pausing only to snatch up his scarlet-lined black cloak from behind the door and, also, to slip his precious *Coffin-Maker's Journal* into his inside pocket, Count Alucard sped out through the door and leapt two at a time down the narrow bedroom stairs.

"Why, Mr Alucard!" gasped Mrs Prendergast, as the vampire Count burst into her kitchen. "What a fright you gave me—"

"Deepest apologies, Mrs Prendergast," broke in the Count. "But there is no time now for explanations. I'm afraid, for both our sakes, I must leave immediately."

"Leave? But you haven't even had your breakfast yet and there's the juiciest grapefruit that you ever clapped eyes on waiting—"

"Hush, dear lady!" hastened the Count, pressing a thin forefinger to Mrs Prendergast's lips as, with his other hand, he placed several Transylvanian banknotes into her palm. "These are to compensate you for any upheaval I may have brought into your life. The reason for my going will shortly be made clear. Try not to think too harshly of me in the years to come, I beg of you. Thank you for all your kindnesses – they have not gone unappreciated, believe me." The Count placed his hand on the worn brass knob on the kitchen door. "Oh, and by the by," he added on an afterthought, "if you should chance to glance inside the wardrobe, you will espy an oblong box I've been obliged to leave behind.

12

You might do me the great favour of keeping an eye on it until I have the opportunity of providing you with a forwarding address. Goodbye, dear lady!"

With which, and with a last well-mannered bow, the Transylvanian Count tugged open the kitchen door and was gone in an instant.

"Well, I never!" gasped old Mrs Prendergast. "I wonder what on earth all that was about?"

But, already, there was the sound of several fists hammering urgently on the front door of the cottage. The old lady would learn, all too quickly, the reason for her lodger's hasty departure.

Count Alucard watched with mixed feelings, from his hiding place behind the graveyard wall, as the postman and the pub's landlord came out of the cottage carrying his coffin on their shoulders.

Minutes before, he had seen the two men march in through the front door, despite Mrs Prendergast's obvious protestations, while the rest of the villagers had remained outside. Now, having satisfied themselves that the unwanted visitor had departed the village, the group turned on their heels, with their scythes, their staves, their other hurtful weapons and their burnt-out smouldering torches, and strode off back the way that they had come, bearing his coffin triumphantly aloft.

At least, the Count told himself, they had left his ex-landlady's cottage unharmed. But what right did they have, he asked himself and with growing anger, to snatch possession of what was not theirs to take?

Alas though, that was the way that it had always been – and always would be, he was very much afraid to say. He had never so much as harmed the smallest of God's living creatures and yet, because he bore the name of his ancestors, he was a hunted and hated man across the whole of Europe.

Perhaps, he told himself, it was time for him to spread wide his bat's wings and fly further afield in search of anonymity and peace? Supposing, for instance, he were to launch himself into the sky and go across the sea to Ireland . . .?

But not at that immediate moment. Although there was no sign of activity along the lane outside old Mrs Prendergast's cottage, the Count knew that it would not be wise to venture out again in daylight. He was aware, from past experience, how quickly rumours spread. Even now, the villagers would be passing the word round the district that there was a vampire at large. For the rest of that day, until the hours of darkness, he would be wise to stay exactly where he was.

Count Alucard settled himself down in the long grass at the edge of the country churchyard and looked at his surroundings. From where he sat, he could see row upon uneven row of carefully tended graves, many of which had stood for centuries and were weather-worn and mossy green. The air was still. There was no sound – except for the soft droning of a distant nectar-seeking bee which was broken, only occasionally, by the song of a pair of crickets serenading each other in the long grass by the churchyard wall.

Count Alucard sighed, happily, and lay out full length on his back, gazing up at a cloudless sky. There was nothing in the whole world he enjoyed

14

quite so much as idling away a few reflective summer hours in a country churchyard – unless it was a full night spent, in his bat form, hanging upside-down in a country church's belfry, gazing up at a sky that was rich with stars.

The Count's day-dreamings were interrupted as a huge jet liner passed directly over his head. The giant aircraft was losing altitude as it headed towards a not-too-far-distant airport. Across the massive, silver fuselage, the Count could plainly read the lettering on the logo:

AMERICAN AIRLINES

"Ah, the United States of America!" mused Count Alucard. "Now, there's a land that judges a fellow for what he is – not what his parents or his grandparents were, or where they came from."

But the USA was thousands of miles away across the great Atlantic Ocean and was much *too* far distant for him even to contemplate as his next destination.

Or was it?

2

"My stars, Hiram P. Hurtzburger!" snapped Hetty Hurtzburger at her famous film producer husband, as she struggled to squeeze into a gold and silver evening gown from out of her jam-packed wardrobe. "If we had to travel by boat, the very least you could have done would have been to get us a bigger cabin than this one!"

"There are people aboard this ship, Hetty, with less cabin space than you have wardrobe!" growled Hiram in reply, juggling his cigar with his lips from one side of his mouth to the other. Hiram P. Hurtzburger was angry not only at his wife, but also at his black bow tie which he was having difficulty, as he always did, in tying. "Gosh darn it, honey!" he continued, "I just don't understand you. We've only got four nights aboard this vessel – would you kindly explain to me why you needed to bring along eleven evening gowns?"

"Because I like to have a choice, Hiram," explained Mrs Hurtzburger, examining her suntan in the dressing-table mirror and carefully patting her blue-rinsed hair into place. "And as for understanding folk – there are times when I find you extremely difficult to make head or tail of? Why couldn't we have *flown* across the Atlantic? On *Concorde*?"

"Aw heck, Hetty!" said Hurtzburger complainingly, untying and then retying the aggravating black bow tie for the umpteenth time. "I've explained all that to you already. We're taking our time in crossing the ocean because I have things I have to *do*, honey." He waved his cigar at a thick stack of typewritten manuscripts on his bedside table. "I need to read all of those movie scripts before we hit New York. If we had crossed on *Concorde*, I wouldn't have had time to read a newspaper."

"Movies, movies, movies! That's all you ever think about, Hiram!" replied Hetty Hurtzburgr tartly, as she tried to decide which shoes to wear out of the twelve pairs she had brought along. "If you hadn't brought so many scripts on this trip," she added, "I could have packed more footwear."

"If I don't make a movie soon that makes a profit, you could very well find yourself going barefoot!" snarled the famous film producer, puffing fiercely on his cigar as his fumbling fingers failed at fastening his bow tie yet again.

For it wasn't just his bow tie and his wife's extravagances that were causing Hiram P. Hurtzburger to lose his temper. Hiram P. Hurtzburger was a worried man. His recent pictures had not been doing at all well. *Frankenstein Goes To Summer School* had lost a packet. *Satan On A Skateboard* had played to empty cinemas all over the world. The box-office takings for his very latest movie, *Oh, Mummy!*, could be described, at best, as wholly disastrous. Hiram P. Hurtzburger had every reason to feel concerned.

"I'll tell you one more thing, Hetty!" snarled the movie mogul, "if I don't find a film to make before this boat docks in New York Harbour, you're going to find a use for all of those shoes you've got inside that wardrobe – we could be *walking* to Los Angeles."

As he spoke, and as if to emphasise his words, the famous film producer flicked his cigar-stub out of the cabin's porthole and then watched as the tiny red glow curved through the night air towards the churning sea below.

The cruise ship had put out from Southampton on that afternoon's tide, only a few short hours before, but already it had left the Isle of Wight behind and was making good speed through the English Channel and towards the open ocean.

"Walk? Did you say *walk*?" Hetty Hurtzburger's voice rose several octaves at the very idea. "Don't be ridiculous, Hiram!" she said, as she eased her chubby frame into the expensive evening-gown. "If we can't afford to fly to Los Angeles, we'll take a yellow cab. Now do stop pretending that we're poverty-stricken, Hiram, and tell me which of these brooches I should wear for the dinner-dance this evening – the one that's studded with sapphires, or the one encrusted with diamonds? . . . Hiram? . . . *Hiram*! Hiram Hurtzburger, are you listening to me?"

"Well, waddaya know about that?" muttered the famous film producer to himself. Mrs Hurtzburger's assumption had been right. Her husband had not heard one word that she had said to him. He was still gazing out through the open porthole into the night. "Hey, Hetty!" he murmured, rubbing the top of his bald head with one hand in some surprise. "Come over here and take a look at this!"

"A look at what?" said Hetty Hurtzburger, rather crossly, as she peered over her husband's shoulder and out through the porthole. "I don't see anything."

"Nope," said the famous film producer. "Neither do I. It's gone now."

"Gone? What's gone? Gone where? Will you stop talking in riddles, Hiram!"

"You're gonna call me a crazy galoot, Hetty," said the famous film producer in tones which suggested that he could scarcely believe his own words

himself, "but I just saw a bat out there."

"A bat? Did you say that you saw a *bat*?"

"I sure did, honey. It flew right past that port-hole."

"Don't be ridiculous, Hiram!" snapped Mrs Hurtzburger. "There are no such things as sea-going bats. It was probably a seagull."

"I tell you, honey, it *was* a bat! A scary bat with big black wings and beady eyes and pointy teeth."

"Hiram Hurtzburger, I'll thank you to remember that this is not a horror movie. We are not in one of your motion picture studios now. We are on board a perfectly respectable liner cruising down the English Channel – and if we don't get a move on, we're going to be late for dinner on our very first night out from port. Now, we wouldn't want that to happen, would we, Hiram?"

"No, honey, but I—"

"Hush up! What is even more important, is that we're sitting at the Captain's table this evening and I, at least, would like to make a good impression – which includes not turning up for dinner when the rest of the guests are halfway through their soup—"

"But, Hetty—"

"Don't interrupt me, Hiram. Listen to me. I shall give you two minutes exactly to fasten your tie, put on your shoes and your white tuxedo, and escort me down to that dining-room. Otherwise, Hiram, I shall go down for dinner by myself and you can order a hamburger in this cabin. Do I make myself clear?"

"Yes, honey," murmured the famous film producer as his nervous fingers reached up to do battle, yet again, with the dangling ends of his tie which hung down on either side of his neck.

The soft strains of the ship's orchestra drifting out through the open portholes of the dining-room, floated across the deck and into a lifeboat where, under the tent-like canvas awning, the stowaway was hidden.

Count Alucard, lying on his back on the lifeboat's wooden planking, slipped his hands underneath the back of his head, listened to the gentle music, and closed his eyes. He was, he had decided, entitled to a few minutes nap at the very least.

The vegetarian vampire had had a very busy day.

The Count's decision, taken that morning, to spend the hours of daylight in the country churchyard had needed to be urgently revised. He had not spent more than ten minutes in the long grass beyond the gravestones when the morning's peace had been shattered suddenly by the noisy stutter of a motor-mower. Bernard Benson, the church's sexton, had taken it into his head to mow the churchyard grass.

Count Alucard had been forced to flee, quickly and quietly, over the churchyard wall. Hugging the bottom of a ditch, he had moved on in search of a different hiding-place. He had spent the rest of that morning and the entire afternoon, hunched in a low brick-built sty which he had had to share with a large, fat-bellied, black-spotted, snuffling, hairy-backed pig. Neither the Count nor the pig had much enjoyed the other's company. But the occasional murmur of voices had forced the Count to stay put.

As soon as dusk had fallen, the Count had bade goodbye to his four-footed, grunting sty-mate and had taken to the road. Moving with deceptively easy strides on his spindly legs, he had made good progress at distancing himself from the unfriendly village. He had travelled no more than a couple of miles when he was again aware of an aircraft's jet engines overhead.

Coming to a halt, Count Alucard stood still and very erect in the middle of the empty country road. Then, taking a tight grip on the edges of his long, black cloak, he threw back his head, spread wide his arms and, in an instant, was transformed into a bat. With one, slow downward sweep of his parchment-like wings, the vegetarian vampire Count launched himself off the ground and into the late evening sky, following the direction taken

22

by the *Lufthansa* jet liner.

Guessing that the *Lufthansa* was going to the continent, the Count headed in its wake. Although he could no longer see the aircraft, the Count was able to take fresh bearings from the pinpoint stars that were beginning to show themselves in the darkening sky.

Flying low, over church steeples, tree tops, farmhouses, fields and hedgerows, he had eventually spotted the narrow ribbon of coastline up ahead and, beyond it, the dark stretch of water that he knew to be the English Channel.

When he had first spotted the lights of the cruise liner, as it ploughed its steady course through the choppy waters, the Count had had no idea of the vessel's destination. However, having flown steadily for well over an hour, he was more than ready to take the opportunity to rest for a while. Swooping down from out of the sky, he had glided at deck-level looking for somewhere to conceal himself for a while.

He had flown over the ship's outdoor swimming pool which had been deserted, as were the deck-game courts and the rows and rows of deckchairs in the observation areas. For he had arrived during that quiet shipboard evening hour when the passengers, for the most part, were either inside their cabins dressing up for dinner in their glad rags (like the Hurtzburgers), or congregating in the ship's several bars enjoying pre-meal, gaily coloured cocktails, in long-stemmed glasses, decorated with tiny parasols and morsels of fruit speared on toothpicks.

Unaware that he had been spotted by one member

of the ship's passenger list, Count Alucard had quickly decided upon the lifeboat's interior as a pleasant place to pass an hour or two unobserved. Having crawled in under the canvas covering, he had turned himself back into his human form and, lulled by the sounds of the ship's orchestra, had quickly nodded off to sleep.

Oddly enough, the music that had sent the Count to sleep was also the cause of his waking up again. It was the sad, sweet strains of several violins that roused him from his slumbers. The evening meal was now over in the dining-room and, while many of the passengers sat sipping at their coffee and nibbling after-dinner mints, some couples were whirling round the small, square dance floor to the strains of a Viennese waltz.

Sitting underneath his canvas awning, Count Alucard listened to the music, and felt sad. But violins always affected the Count that way. They reminded him of Transylvania, and of pine forests, and smoky camp-fires by moonlight, and brightly coloured gypsy caravans . . . The sound of violins made Count Alucard feel homesick. He also felt, at that particular moment, as if he was without a friend in the entire world . . .

Taking a large, spotted handkerchief from out of his trouser pocket, Count Alucard wiped a tear from his cheek and then blew his nose, twice, loudly.

Come along, he told himself! This wouldn't do at all! This was no way for a member of the Transylvanian aristocracy to behave. Feeling sorry for himself was not going to help the situation one little bit. No, he would need to pull himself together. After

24

all, things weren't *too* bad, were they? At least he was undiscovered *and* under cover. The lifeboat's wood planking had provided him with a hard bed – but if he were to look around, perhaps he might come across some spare canvas he could use for a mattress and, maybe, a lifejacket that would serve as a pillow . . .?

Yes, looking on the brighter side, things could be a whole lot worse! Why, he might even choose to spend a couple of nights underneath the canvas awning. The lifeboat would make quite a comfortable temporary home for him before he chose to take to his bat's wings again. There was, of course, the question of food. But surely, on a ship of this size, it should not prove too difficult to find something to eat? Once the passengers had taken to their cabins, he could search the dining-room for leftovers . . .

The Count paused in his musings as something slightly disturbing occurred to him. There was a rather distasteful smell coming from somewhere close at hand . . .

Count Alucard sniffed, deeply. He wrinkled his nose in some disgust and then forced himself to sniff again.

Oh, no!

The unpleasant odour, he discovered, was coming from himself! Or, to be more exact, from the sole of one of his shoes. During his afternoon spent in the pigsty, it seemed that he had inadvertently trodden in some pig-dirt. A quantity of that foul-smelling substance was now attached to the sole of his black patent leather right shoe. There was even a

25

little of it on the left shoe too!

Pooh!

Count Alucard pulled a face. In the close confines of the lifeboat, the awful smell seemed to be getting worse. It might be necessary, he told himself, to take a stroll around the ship's decks sooner rather than later – not only to go in search of something to eat but also in order to get away from the horrible stench . . .

"A *bat*?" Captain Humphrey Summerhouse, the tall, handsome master of the cruise ship, *Orvatelle*, tried to hide his amusement as he looked across the empty coffee-cups and discarded after-dinner mint wrapping-papers at the portly, bald-headed American passenger whose name he couldn't remember. "Did you say a *bat*?"

"It flew right past my porthole," replied Hiram P. Hurtzburger, in some embarrassment. He realised that several of the other passengers seated around the captain's table were looking at him rather oddly. He was aware, also, of the angry look that his wife was flashing him for mentioning the subject. "I could see its beady eyes and its pointy teeth," he added, rather lamely.

"I'm afraid you must have been mistaken, Mr . . . er . . . er—"

"Hurtzburger," snapped the famous film producer. "Hiram P. Hurtzburger's my name – and I am here to tell you that I know what I saw— Ouch!" he added, as Mrs Hurtzburger kicked his ankle, hard, underneath the table.

"There are no bats on this ship, Mr Hamburger,"

26

the captain continued, bestowing a smile on all the lady passenger guests seated around the table, as he added, jokingly: "Unless you count the table tennis bats in the games room!"

His last remark was greeted with polite titters of laughter from the ladies, all of whom were full of admiration for the sea captain's rugged good looks and were keen to make an impression on him on this first night out from port.

"Table tennis bats indeed!" chortled a thin-faced, aristocratic-looking lady who was festooned with diamonds. She fluttered her eyelashes at the captain as she gazed over the rim of her coffee-cup which was held, delicately, betwixt forefinger and thumb, and added: "That's the funniest thing I ever heard in all my life! Table tennis bats! I say!"

"Not half as funny, Lady Fossington-Twiste, as the thought of real live bats aboard the *Orvatelle*," smirked the captain, who liked a compliment.

"Why, do look, everybody!" cried Mrs Hurtz- burger, trying to steer the conversation away from bats of any description. "Who, for heaven's sakes, is that dreamy looking guy over there by the fruit?"

Captain Summerhouse, and the other passengers seated at his table, turned and looked across the ship's dance floor towards a long table, covered with a pink tablecloth, and which contained all that was left of that evening's dessert: an enormous cut glass bowl containing a half-eaten sherry trifle decorated with *glacé* cherries; less than half of a huge walnut and cream *gâteau*; two individual *crème caramels*, and a giant-sized wickerwork basket piled high with apples, pears, oranges, bananas, nectarines, two pineapples and lots and lots of grapes.

Standing close by the fruit basket and gazing at it, hungrily, stood a tall, thin, pale-faced man with jet-black hair slicked straight back over his head. He was dressed in a black suit, a starched, white shirt with a wing-collar, a black bow tie and had a gold medallion suspended on a chain around his neck.

"I say! What a fascinating looking man!" said Lady Fossington-Twiste, who had put on a pair of diamond-studded spectacles which matched her earrings, her necklace, and the gems that sparkled similarly on her fingers. "Do summon him over, this instant, Captain, and introduce us."

"I'm afraid I am unable to do that, Lady Fossington-Twiste," replied Captain Summerhouse, rather coldly, for he always preferred to be the centre of attention himself. "I'm afraid I don't know who he is – I have not had time, as yet, to study the passenger list." Rising to his feet, the ship's captain smiled at his evening's dinner table guests. "And now, if you'll excuse me, ladies and gentlemen, I'm afraid that I must leave you. I have to be on the bridge early in the morning. Goodnight, everybody!"

The male passengers mumbled their 'goodnights' back at the captain as he moved away, but the ladies gathered around the table stayed silent, their eyes still firmly fixed on the strange, sad-faced, tall, thin man standing over by the dessert table.

Count Alucard ran the tip of his tongue over the inside of his top lip as he stared at the juicy, fat deep-purple grapes. He was wondering if he might manage to slip some of the tempting fruit into his

28

pocket and then make a hasty exit before anyone had noticed he had entered the dining-room.

Strolling around the near-deserted deck some moments earlier, he had spotted the overburdened basket of fruit through an open porthole. Having not eaten all day, he had summoned his courage and strode in through the doors intent on purloining a morsel or two and taking it back to the privacy of the lifeboat.

He reached out with his long fingers and had just broken off a stem containing some dozen or so of the richest-coloured, ripest-looking of the grapes when, to his horror, a voice spoke into his ear.

"Excuse me, but might I have a word?"

The vampire Count gulped, hastily stuffed the cluster of grapes into his right hand trouser pocket, and turned to find himself confronted by a thin-faced, keen-eyed lady who seemed to be sparkling with diamonds.

"Pardon me for asking," continued Lady Fossington-Twiste, "but haven't we met somewhere before?"

"I . . . I . . . I don't think that I have had that pleasure, dear lady," stammered the Count, wishing that he had not allowed the pangs of hunger to tempt him into entering the ship's dining-room.

"Oh, but I believe we have, you know." The aristocratic lady knew full well that she had never before set eyes on the tall, thin, dark-eyed stranger, but she had crossed the dance floor from the Captain's table, intent on making his acquaintance. "Could it have been at last year's Royal Garden Party?" she continued. "Didn't we share a joke

29

together with a certain royal person, over a plate of bite-size sausage rolls?"

"Alas, no," murmured the Count, shaking his head. "I'm afraid I didn't attend that regal function."

"How strange. Do you know, I would have sworn on oath that we gave some cherry-cake crumbs, together, to the royal corgis. I'm Lady Fossington-Twiste, by the by. Who did you say you were again?"

"Alucard. Count Alucard," said the Transylvanian vampire Count, forgetting himself momentarily and then immediately biting his tongue at having revealed his identity.

Luckily, the name and title meant nothing to his questioner. "Alucard . . .? Alucard . . .?" Lady Fossington-Twiste repeated the name, thoughtfully, and then continued: "I don't think I know the Alucards? I met some Alucazzis once, in Florence, I don't suppose . . .?"

"No, no, no . . ." The Count's eyes roamed around the dining-room, frantically, as he sought to change the conversation. The main lights had dimmed above the small, polished-wood dance area, which was now lit by overhead hanging strings of fairy lights in twinkling colours. The orchestra was still playing, softly now, and only two or three couples were drifting round the dance floor. "Would you care to dance, dear lady?" asked the Count in some desperation.

"How very kind of you to offer," replied Lady Fossington-Twiste, her eyes sparkling as brilliantly as her diamonds in anticipation.

Count Alucard led his partner onto the dance floor where he put one arm around her waist and took her hand in his. They set out, slowly at first, around the floor and to the doleful sound of saxophones. But the vampire Count was an accomplished ballroom dancer and his companion seemed to grow in confidence under his assured guidance.

Then, as the ship's orchestra changed the tempo from that of a slow foxtrot to a lively Latin number, the Transylvanian Count whirled Lady Fossington-Twiste round and around, to and fro, back and forth. The other dancing couples, respectful of this display, left the floor in order that the pair could better show off their skills. When the number came to its end, the passengers seated at the tables broke out into spontaneous and enthusiastic applause.

Count Alucard bowed, modestly, four times and in four different directions. For a couple of minutes, at least, under the twinkling fairy lights and lost in the music, he had forgotten his troubles and imagined himself in happier times now gone, attending some grand function in the splendour of the Castle Alucard's ballroom, in the days before the villagers had stormed his home and burned it to the ground.

The Count sighed, softly, to himself and then turned and smiled at his dancing partner. "Thank you, dear lady," he said gravely.

"Not at all, the pleasure was entirely mine," fluttered Lady Fossington-Twiste, still a trifle breathless after being whirled round the dance floor. Then, wrinkling her nose, she added: "But tell me, Count, did you detect a curious odour during our dance?"

"An odour, dear lady?" said the Count, gulping slightly as he suddenly recollected what it was that had driven him from the comparative safety of the lifeboat. In his enjoyment of the dance, he had quite forgotten the awful stench that came from the stuff that had got attached to the soles of his shoes in the pigsty.

"Yes. A sort of unpleasant farmyardy odour. It seemed to follow us around."

"I didn't notice anything out of the ordinary," said the Count – but now that his dancing partner had mentioned it, he realised that the disgusting smell was attacking his own nostrils once more.

"I did," said the puzzled Lady Fossington-Twiste. "I can smell it now. In fact, it seems to be getting stronger all the time. I wonder where it's coming from?" She shuddered slightly with disgust, causing her earrings to twinkle as they shimmered with the reflections of a hundred flashing fairy lights.

"No, no – I can't smell anything out of the ordinary," said the Count, shaking his head and then continuing quickly: "If you will excuse me, dear lady, I'm afraid I must fly . . . *dash*," he added, correcting his unfortunate choice of word. "Goodnight!"

With which, Count Alucard turned and strode quickly out of the ship's dining-room to be swallowed up by the dark night.

"He's the Count Alucard. I've met him before," lied Lady Fossington-Twiste, as soon as she had rejoined her dinner-table companions. "We shared a plate of nibbles together at last year's Royal Garden Party."

"A real live *count*?" said Hetty Hurtzburger, enviously. "Do you think he might care to make up a four at deck tennis one morning?"

"Is he travelling first class?" enquired a second lady.

"Of course he's travelling first class," snorted a third. "You surely don't imagine that a count would travel anything less than *first*?"

"I don't see why not," objected a fourth. "*I* once knew a duke who hadn't got a penny to his name."

The conversation regarding the financial state of Lady Fossington-Twiste's dancing partner continued around the Captain's table for several minutes with everyone arguing animatedly. Everyone, that is, except Hiram P. Hurtzburger, the famous film producer, who had sat quietly, doodling with his pen on the menu card, having had nothing to say for himself since he had been ridiculed regarding his sighting of the bat outside his cabin porthole.

It was Hurtzburger though who eventually brought the small talk to an abrupt stop.

"Say, will you folks button up your lips for a moment!" he snapped. "I can't hardly hear myself think." Then, as his fellow passengers blinked in some surprise at this rude interruption, he turned to Lady Fossington-Twiste. "What was that dude called? Did you say 'Alucard'?"

"Count Alucard," simpered Lady Fossington-Twiste, and she fluttered her hands in the air like a young girl, as she added: "Isn't it just the dreamiest sounding name?"

"Dreamiest?" growled Hurtzburger. "If you ask me, it's more like a nightmare!"

The passengers sitting round the table exchanged puzzled glances as Hurtzburger, who, instead of explaining his last remark, took a fat cigar out of the top pocket of his dinner-jacket, bit off the end and then lit the cigar with a gold cigarette-lighter which was engraved in fancy lettering with the monogram 'H.P.H.'. He puffed on the cigar for several seconds before blowing a cloud of blue smoke across the table, savouring the surprise he had in store. As a film producer, Hiram P. Hurtzburger knew the value of suspense.

"Haven't any of you got sufficient knowhow to realise that 'Alucard' is 'Dracula' back to front?" said Hurtzburger at last, displaying the name which he had written on his menu card.

There was a moment's stunned silence during which the guests that were seated around that table dwelled separately on the thought that there *had* been something rather strange about the tall, dark foreign-looking gentleman who had whirled Lady Fossington-Twiste around the small, polished square of dance floor.

"B-b-b-but surely that's just coincidence?" said a male guest nervously.

"Oh, yeah?" sneered Hurtzburger, jabbing at the air with his cigar as he spoke in order to emphasize his words. "And I guess the furry, black bat with the pointy teeth outside my porthole was just coincidence too?"

The passengers addressed reacted in different ways to Hurtzburger's reminder of his earlier statement: some of them gasped; others twitched their heads nervously; several more of them shook visibly;

35

one lady's knuckles showed white as she gripped tight on the pink tablecloth.

"C'mon, honey," snapped Hurtzburger to his wife, as he pulled himself to his feet. "It's my opinion that there's a blood-drinking monster on board this ship! In which circumstance, the safest place to be is inside our cabin with the door locked tight."

This time, Hetty Hurtzburger did not question her husband's words. Dutifully, she rose, pushed back her chair and followed him towards the open door which led out onto the promenade deck.

The passengers remaining around the captain's table shot each other nervous glances, each waiting for another to take the lead. It was Lady Fossington-Twiste who was the first to move. As the full horror of the situation gradually dawned upon her, she got slowly to her feet, her face deathly pale.

"I danced with Dracula!" she wailed in a high-pitched voice which travelled all around the room, silencing the conversation at the other tables. It was sufficient to cause consternation among the musicians, bringing their dance music to a sudden stop. "I was partnered by a blood-drinking vampire!" she continued, her bejewelled fingers feeling all around her neck as she sought to reassure herself that the Count hadn't snatched at opportunity and taken a sly nip at her throat during their perambulations on the dance floor.

"Dracula is somewhere at large aboard this vessel!" she shouted out dramatically. Then, partly out of relief at finding herself unharmed, but mostly as a late reaction to her horrible experience, she collapsed suddenly in a dead faint on to her chair, her head falling forward on to the tablecloth.

There was pandemonium then in the dining-room as passengers, musicians and waiters alike, rushed hither and thither in their attempts to follow the example set by the Hurtzburgers and seek the safety of their separate cabins.

3

"Captain! Captain!"

"What's the matter?" called Captain Summerhouse, rather impatiently, at the sound of the stew-
ard's anxious voice outside his door, accompanied
by the urgent hammering of his fists. There were
other sounds too, the captain realised: running footsteps and more raised voices from several parts of
the ship.

"The First Officer asked me to fetch you, sir!"
cried Able-Seaman Arthur Treadwell. "You're
wanted up on deck!"

"All right, all right!" replied the captain, testily.
"Tell him I'll be along directly!"

"Very good, sir!" Outside the captain's cabin, the
sailor paused for a moment to pull a face. There was
a rather nasty smell coming from somewhere close
at hand. A smell which he could not quite put his
finger on, but which had no difficulty in making its
way up Treadwell's nostrils.

"Pooh! What a dreadful niff!" said the sailor to
himself. But there was no time now for him to seek
out the source of the awful pong – he knew that
there were more important matters in hand. Arthur
Treadwell turned and moved off quickly along the

corridor, back the way that he had come.

Inside the cabin, Captain Summerhouse slipped a tasselled bookmark between the pages of *Treasure Island*, the book he was reading in bedtime instalments, and swung his bare feet onto the cosily carpeted floor.

It really wasn't good enough, the captain grumbled to himself as he crossed towards the door in his striped pyjamas. He had just been getting to his favourite part of *Treasure Island*– those thrilling moments when the cabin-boy, Jim Hawkins, hides inside the apple-barrel – when he had been rudely interrupted by the summons from his First Officer. And on the first night out at sea. No, it really wasn't good enough at all! And, in all probability, it would turn out to be just another false alarm.

The same thing had happened, a week before, when they had sailed for Southampton from New York. On that occasion, he had been reading the beginning of *Treasure Island* – the exciting bit where Jim discovers the treasure map – when his First Officer had summoned him from his bed and up onto the bridge. And all because, it had turned out, one of the ship's cooks had misplaced his jelly-mould!

Well, if it was something equally trifling this time, the First Officer would be in serious trouble, Captain Summerhouse promised himself—

"Pooh! What a disgusting stink!" the captain spoke out loud as he opened his cabin door. Then, as he stooped to pick up the pair of shoes he had placed ouside to be polished by the night-steward, he realised where the awful stench was coming from

– it was from the shoes themselves!

He picked them up, distastefully, between finger and thumb and, on turning them over discovered, as he had suspected, that there was some sort of foul substance sticking to the soles of both of the shoes. But what? It couldn't be dog-dirt because dogs were strictly forbidden aboard ship. Inspecting the shoes as closely as the stench allowed – at arm's length – the captain made another discovery: the shoes weren't even his!

Someone had taken his shoes and left him this foul-smelling pair in their place. But who would dare to do such a thing? And *why*?

Captain Summerhouse knew neither the identity of the wrongdoer, nor the motive for the unpleasant crime – but he took grim comfort in promising himself that when he did lay hands on the culprit, he would give him good cause to regret the deed.

Back in the safety of the canvas-covered lifeboat, Count Alucard smiled as he pulled the largest, juiciest grape off the stalk and popped it into his mouth. His expression changed immediately to one of distaste as he spat out the grape. It wasn't real. It was made of plastic.

So that was why the fruit-basket had been full to overflowing while the other puddings and desserts had been mostly eaten. The wickerwork basket and its luscious-looking contents were purely decorative. Oh well, at least his venture out and about the ship had not been entirely unsuccessful.

The Count stretched out his legs in front of him and admired his new non-niffy shoes. Not only was there no unpleasant odour attached to them, they were also a perfect fit. He was a little sad that he had been forced to resort to theft in order to replace his footwear, but he had been driven by necessity. There was no way that he could have spent the entire night in the close confines of the lifeboat, with a pair of shoes that gave off such an awful stink.

As for the fact that he was hungrier now than ever, perhaps in an hour or so, when the passengers and most of the crew were asleep, he might just venture out again in search of the ship's kitchens. There was a half-eaten sherry trifle somewhere on board still, to say nothing of almost half a very large walnut and cream gateau . . .

But that would have to wait for a while. At the moment, he could hear sounds of people moving about around the ship and, also, the hubbub of voices. In fact, when he listened very carefully, the Count was puzzled to discover that there seemed to be more noise now than there had been earlier. Which was strange, considering the lateness of the hour. Although the Count was not aware, as yet, that he himself was the cause of all the unrest he decided, just to be on the safe side, that the best thing he could do would be to lay low for at least an hour . . .

"Quiet, please! Order, order!" called out Captain Summerhouse, banging at the same time on the bass drum in an attempt to still the chattering in the ship's dining-room.

Although it was now well past midnight, the room was packed to overflowing with both passengers and members of the crew, all of them worried about the reported presence of a vampire on board the vessel. When it had been proposed that a meeting should be held in order to discuss the vampire situation, word had travelled quickly and the dining-room had been filled in minutes. The original decision to seek the safety of their separate cabins, with the doors securely locked, had given way, as panic spread throughout the ship, to a general feeling that there was safety in numbers.

But there was an air of unease in the dining-room. Some of the passengers still wore their evening clothes while others, having been roused hastily from their bunks, had dressing-gowns over their pyjamas or nightdresses. Some of the sailors, lacking dressing-gowns, wore raincoats over their usual night attire.

There were some even less appropriately dressed. Nigel Fairweather, the ship's purser, who had been taking a latenight shower when the alarm was raised, was wearing only a large Donald Duck bath-towel round his middle and was still carrying a big loofah which, in his haste, he had neglected to leave behind.

Captain Summerhouse frowned as he caught sight

of his ship's purser who was standing near the door of the dining-room. The captain noted, too, that Fairweather was dripping on the carpet. Trust him, thought Summerhouse, to let the ship's company down.

Summerhouse had made sure that he himself was dressed properly for the occasion: trousers neatly pressed, jacket buttons gleaming gold, his gold-braided captain's cap sitting jauntily on his head. Captain Summerhouse's impeccable turnout was intended as a reassuring sight for the nervous company assembled in the dining-room. By positioning himself on the orchestra's platform, just behind the drum kit, he was managing to conceal the fact that he was wearing a pair of well-worn tartan carpet slippers instead of his usual black, shiny shoes.

It had not been until after he had thrust the pair of smelly shoes out through his porthole, into the sea, that Captain Summerhouse had remembered, to his horror, that he had left his spare pair of black shoes back at home on this voyage, in order that Mrs Summerhouse might take them to be soled-and-heeled.

He wriggled his toes inside the offending slippers. Unless he could borrow a pair of shoes from one of the ship's officers – or unless the stolen pair turned up – he would be forced to captain the ship for the next few days in the hideous tartan slippers, which he had never cared for and which had been a Christmas gift, some years before, from an unfavourite aunt.

All the same, Summerhouse told himself, he had made some sort of an effort in the present crisis. He had done his best. No man can ever do more. It was at times like these that he and his fellow officers were expected to set some sort of an example to the passengers and the crew. Fairweather had made a complete fool of himself. Captain Summerhouse made a mental note to speak quite severely to the purser the very next morning. Meanwhile, there was a very tense situation that demanded all of his attention.

"If you will all keep calm, I'm sure we'll soon have the matter under control!" announced the captain, holding up his hands for silence as the murmurs grew louder around the dining-room. "There's really nothing to worry about," he added.

"Isn't there indeed!" barked a heavily built red-faced man with a big moustache who looked as though he might have been an ex-army officer. "You might think that having a blood-drinking vampire on board your ship is not a cause for concern, sir – but we passengers think otherwise."

"Hear! hear!" said a small man in a piping voice, who was sitting just behind the red-faced, big-moustached man.

"What we need to know," cried a third man who was sitting in the front row, "is whether or not the crew are armed and trained to deal with such a situation?"

"Hear! hear!" piped up the small man.

"What about the women and children?" shouted a tall, earnest looking chap who had a beard and was wearing a roll-neck pullover. "Why don't you lower the lifeboats now and put our wives and children into them?"

This time there was no piping voice to be heard and the captain guessed that the small man probably had neither wife nor children and was concerned only for his own safety. But the murmurs of fear and discontent were again increasing in volume and the captain was forced to beat the drum once more before he was able to make himself heard.

Boom-boom-*BOOM!*

"Order, *please!*" bellowed Captain Summerhouse. "There's no call for panic. After all, we don't know yet for certain that there *is* a vampire on board. I, for one, would like to be convinced of that. All we do know is that one passenger says he saw a bat outside his porthole while another says she danced with a man who said he was Count Alucard. Do they sound sufficient reasons for lowering the lifeboats?"

" 'Alucard'," announced the bearded man in the roll-neck pullover, "is 'Dracula' back to front."

"I realise that," snapped the Captain. "And I'm not proposing that we do nothing. I intend to organise search-parties and have this ship examined from prow to stern. Be sure that if there is a vampire on board, we'll find him. Now then, I already have the crew-members – but do any of you passengers wish to volunteer?"

One by one, taking courage from the captain's call for action, the passengers began to raise their hands.

"You'll need to provide the search-parties with stakes," called out the man in the roll-neck pullover while all of this was going on.

"I know exactly what I need to do," snapped the captain, who was beginning to think that the chap in the roll-neck pullover was a bit of a know-it-all. "I'm not sure that there are enough steaks on board though – I was going to ask the ship's cooks to rustle up some cheese and tomato sandwiches for everyone later on."

"No, no, no!" replied the man in the roll-neck pullover, his beard bristling with excitement. "I said 'stakes', not 'steaks'. *Wooden* stakes. Pointed ones. The only way to kill a vampire is to drive a sharp wooden stake though its evil heart."

"I know that," lied the captain. "I was going to ask the ship's carpenter to make us some."

"And mallets!" called out the military-looking man, fiercely. "We'll need wooden mallets if we're going to bang the stakes through the monster's heart!"

"Hear! hear!" the small man piped up, eagerly.

"I don't think we've got any wooden mallets on board," said the captain doubtfully. He was beginning to sense a change of mood in the dining-room. The previous feeling of fear was evaporating fast and being replaced by a general bloodthirsty desire to hunt down the vampire. He wasn't altogether sure that this was a good thing. Supposing the search-parties, in their enthusiasm, went on the rampage with pointed stakes and wooden mallets? They might start hammering the stakes into the very first person that they came across. And, certainly, if they should chance to bump into this Alucard chap, they would hammer first and ask questions afterwards, whether he happened to be a vampire or no. The captain shivered at the thought. After all, he told himself, he was the one who was in charge of the ship. If anyone on board should happen to get a wooden stake hammered into them without just cause, he would be the one to answer for it. No, the thing to do would be to proceed with caution. "I'm absolutely certain that there aren't any mallets anywhere on board," he continued, firmly, and added: "In which circumstance I think we should proceed with caution and—"

Captain Summerhouse broke off as, out of the corner of his eye, he became aware of someone waving a loofah at him from across the dining-room. Turning in that direction, he realised that it was the purser, Fairweather, who was holding his Donald Duck towel round his middle with one hand, while waving the loofah with the other.

"Yes, purser?" the captain continued, rather coldly. Trust Fairweather, he told himself, not only to turn up wearing nothing but a silly towel but also to draw attention to himself.

"Please, Captain, we have got some mallets on the ship. Plenty of them. They're up on the games deck. We use them for deck croquet."

"I was well aware of that fact, thank you, Fairweather," said the captain, trying hard to contain his anger. He might have known, he told himself, that Fairweather would put his foot in it! "But as it happens," he continued aloud, "I didn't think that they were quite the type of mallet we were looking for – they've got long handles for one thing, and for another—"

But, already, several of the passengers and some of the more excitable crew-members were on their feet and looking for the exits.

"They'll do for us!" cried the military-looking man as he led the rush towards the deck outside. "We can saw the handles down to size. This way! Tally-ho! Let's kill the black-hearted villain!"

BOOM-BOOM-BOOM! Captain Summerhouse banged on the drum as loudly as he could in order to halt the tide of departing passengers and crew-members.

"Wait!" cried the captain as the vampire-hunters halted, temporarily, at the sound of the drum. "Before we do anything hasty – wouldn't it be best to question both of the eyewitnesses first? An exact description of this Count Alucard chap might come in handy, before anyone went looking for him. And, if I was going out on deck, in the dark, I'd like to hear a bit more about this vampire bat, before *it* came looking for me – with its black, beady eyes and its sharp, pointy teeth."

The party of men who had made eagerly for the door hesitated now, shuffled their feet and exchanged anxious glances. Perhaps the captain was right. There was no sense in rushing into anything without knowing exactly the nature of the beast with which they were about to tangle.

"Is Lady Fossington-Twiste here?" said the captain, playing for time and looking around the dining-room. "And, if so, would she stand up, please?"

But there was no sign of that bejewelled person in the room. Neither did anyone else present seem to be aware of the titled lady's whereabouts. Except for one man. Captain Summerhouse had caught sight, again, of a raised loofah making wiggling signs at him.

"Yes, Mr Fairweather?" he said, icily.

"I think that Lady Fossington-Twiste was taken ill," said the purser. "She had to be assisted down to the sick bay."

"I'll bet Dracula sank his fangs into her!" cried a sailor who was one of the volunteer search-party.

"For all we know," growled the red-faced military-looking man, waving aloft a dangerous looking pepper-mill he had acquired, "the poor woman's probably dead."

"No, you don't die exactly if you're bitten by a vampire," said the bearded know-it-all in the roll-neck pullover. "You *sort of* die – but you're not really dead. You turn deathly white and become a vampire yourself – with bloodshot eyes and pointy teeth," he paused, to give the assembled company time to silently digest these words and then added, offhandedly: "It's as bad as being dead – worse, probably."

The awesome hush was broken, almost instantly, as the angry murmurs started up again, accompanied by several angry shouts from some of the members of the search-party.

"Let's get out there and get him!" growled one of the volunteers.

"Aye-aye, lads!" cried a heavily-built sailor. "Let's drive those stakes into the foul fiend's heart!"

"Follow me!" commanded the red-faced soldierly-like man, brandishing the big pepper-mill above his head. "We'll give the blighter what for!"

BOOM-BOOM-BOOM!

"Wait! *Wait*!" called Captain Summerhouse and, as the search-party hovered impatiently, he wondered how his hero, Captain Livesey, on board *Treasure Island's* good ship *Hispaniola*, would have dealt with the situation. "At least wait until we've got a description of this bat! Would passenger Hurtzburger stand up, please?"

But, apart from the turning heads of a few inquisitive passengers as they sought to catch a glimpse of the man who had seen the vampire bat outside his porthole, there was no movement in the ship's dining-room. Of Hiram P. Hurtzburger himself there was no sign.

"Mr Hurtzburger?" called out the captain for a second time.

Again there came no reply.

"Do you think that Dracula's got him?" asked a lady passenger, casting a nervous glance towards the night outside.

"Not a doubt about it!" snapped the military-looking gentleman who was hovering impatiently by the exit. "What are we waiting for? Let's go and get that vampire now!"

Then, with his moustache bristling fiercely and waving the enormous pepper-mill above his head, he led a stampede out through the dining-room doors. Once outside and standing on the moonlit deck, the military-looking gentleman detailed off the search-party into two separate and sizeable groups – one to go and collect the croquet mallets; the other to set about finding pointed bits of wood or metal that would serve as stakes to be driven into Dracula's heart.

"But don't go wandering off in ones and twos," he warned them. "Stick together, whatever you do!

There's a sharp-toothed, evil-hearted monster at large and roaming this vessel, intent on slaking its thirst with blood – don't let it be yours!"

With these fearful words ringing in their ears, the two groups set off across the deck in opposite directions.

Left alone with the women passengers, their children, and the more faint-hearted of the passengers and crew-members, Captain Summerhouse listened to the separate sets of footsteps running off into the night. He scowled across the room and in the general direction of the purser. It was, to some extent, all Fairweather's fault, the captain told himself. If only his purser had kept his mouth shut about the croquet mallets, the search-party might never have set foot outside the dining-room.

"Captain Summerhouse?"

Having noted that the captain was looking across in his direction, Nigel Fairweather had lifted up his loofah and wiggled it yet again.

"What is it this time, Fairweather?" snapped Summerhouse, bad-temperedly.

"Oh, nothing, sir," murmured the purser, hitching up the bath-towel which would insist on slipping down round his middle and wondering, the while, why the captain seemed so cross with him? "I was just wondering, sir, if you would like me to go and see if I can organize those cheese and tomato sandwiches you mentioned earlier – for the women and children?"

"I don't care what you do, Fairweather, provided that you get rid of that ridiculous bath-towel and into your uniform!"

"Very good, sir," mumbled the purser, moving towards the door with the uncomfortable feeling that all eyes were firmly fixed, if not upon himself, upon the gaily coloured Donald Duck at present attached to his person.

"Fairweather!"

"Sir?" The purser paused, turned and looked across enquiringly at the captain who was still standing on the orchestra platform.

"You might keep your eyes peeled for passenger Hurtzburger while you're wandering about the ship. He's the one who started all this palaver about there being a vampire on board."

"Yes, sir!" said the purser and, as he spoke, he lifted up the loofah in a sort of half-salute.

Captain Summerhouse sighed, shook his head and wiggled his toes, angrily, in his tartan-slippers, as he watched Fairweather padding barefooted out of the dining-room. He hoped though that the purser might be able to make contact with the Hurtzburger fellow. Hurtzburger and Fairweather between them had a great deal to answer for. Hurtzburger, Fairweather and that other fellow with the pepper-mill who looked as if he ought to be in the army . . . Mostly though – and perhaps a little unfairly – Captain Summerhouse laid the blame at Fairweather's door. But what else was one to expect, he asked himself, of a ship's officer who turned up in an emergency dressed only in a Donald Duck bath-towel and carrying a loofah?

4

"My stars, Hiram Hurtzburger!" hissed Hetty Hurtzburger as the knocking continued on the door of their cabin. "Don't you think that we ought to at least find out who it is?"

But her famous film producer husband shook his head and shot his wife a silencing glance as the heavy hammering on the door continued.

"Hello?" said the voice from the corridor. "Is anybody at home? Are you in there, Mr Hurtzburger? Because, if you are, Captain Summerhouse would like a word with you."

Hetty Hurtzburger, both puzzled and angry at her husband's refusal to answer the door, glared at him across the cabin. But Hiram P. Hurtzburger returned Hetty's frown with a secretive smile and placed a forefinger to the side of his mouth which did not contain his cigar. Some moments later, when all seemed quiet outside the cabin, the film producer tiptoed to the door, opened it gently, and peered along the corridor at the retreating figure.

"Well, Hiram?" demanded Hetty as her husband reclosed the door as softly as he had opened it. "Did you see who it was?"

"Some nut wearing nothing but a bath-towel,"

replied Hiram with a shrug and without taking the cigar from out of his mouth.

"But suppose it was important?" snapped Mrs Hurtzburger. "If the captain wants to see you – don't you think you should find out why exactly?"

"Nope!" replied the film producer firmly. "He may want to see me, honey – but I have gotten no desire whatsoever to set eyes on him. Not until I have made contact with a certain other gentleman first." With which, Hurtzburger reopened the cabin door and glanced again along the corridor outside, this time to make sure that the coast was clear. It was. "Lock the door behind me, Hetty, and don't open it to anyone until I get back."

"But, Hiram, you can't leave me here all alone!" gasped the horrified Hetty Hurtzburger as she realized that her husband intended to go out. "Not with a vampire roaming round the ship!"

"Believe me, honey, you'll be okay," Hurtzburger attempted to reassure his wife. "I'll be back before you know I'm gone."

"Where are you going, Hiram? What *for*?"

"Just up on deck, honey. On urgent business."

"Urgent business!" wailed Mrs Hurtzburger. "Look at the time, Hiram. It's well past midnight and we're out at sea. What urgent business do you have on board a ship and in the middle of the night?"

"Movie business," said her husband mysteriously, adding: "Just trust me, Hetty, that's all I ask. And if this deal works out, honey, when we get back to Los Angeles, I'll buy you the biggest diamond bracelet in Beverly Hills."

56

Then, before Hetty Hurtzburger had time to utter one further word in protest, Hiram slipped out into the corridor, closing the door behind him and leaving, in his wake, a fast disappearing spiral of blue cigar smoke.

"Biggest diamond bracelet in Beverly Hills, my eye!" Hetty Hurtzburger murmured softly to herself as she slipped home the bolt on her cabin door, for safety, before sitting down despondently on her bed.

For it was by no means the first time that the famous film producer's wife had heard promises of that kind and, on each and every previous occasion, they had evaporated into thin air – just like Hiram's blue cigar smoke.

When Hiram P. Hurtzburger had been filming *Frankenstein Goes To Summer School*, he faithfully promised Hetty that, as soon as the movie was in profit, they would move into the swishest house in the poshest part of Hollywood. Alas though, instead of making money the movie had lost a packet and, instead of moving into a grander home than the one that they already lived in, they were forced to move into a slightly *less* grand one with – horror of horrors! – a slightly smaller swimming pool.

During the making of *Satan On A Skateboard*, Hiram had promised Hetty, with his hand on his heart, that when the movie was completed he would buy her a brand new Beverly Hills wardrobe which would make her the envy of all the other Hollywood producers' wives. But *Satan On A Skateboard* had proved more of a disaster than the previous movie and Hetty, instead of finding herself the envy of her friends, had been forced to hide behind the shrubbery at several Hollywood parties, rather than disclose that she was wearing the same old expensive gowns and costly dresses that they had seen before.

When they had been on location in the desert with his last picture, *Oh, Mummy!*, pestered by flies and beggars, Hiram had assured Hetty that, in recompense, she would attend the movie's glitzy New York premiere wearing the finest new mink coat that money could buy . . . Unfortunately, as things turned out, *Oh, Mummy!* had proved such an awful film that it had been premiered not in New York but in a tiny fishing town in northern Nova Scotia. The only fur coats to be seen that night were on the backs of a couple of rather scruffy Eskimos who, in company with most of the audience, had left the cinema before the movie was halfway through . . .

Sitting in the comfort of her first class cabin, gazing sadly at her image in the dressing-room mirror which gazed equally sadly back, Hetty Hurtzburger sighed as she pondered on her unsatisfactory lifestyle.

There was nothing worse, Hetty told herself, than being very rich instead of *very*, very rich. She was not an unfeeling woman. She pitied the poor people of the world and contributed generously, whenever she was asked, to all kinds of charities. But at least the poor were all in the same boat. They had got each other. But when you were only partway rich, it meant that you lived a life surrounded by people much richer than you were yourself. It was *very* frustrating.

It was frustrating too to be married to a man who

took himself off, in the middle of the night, on yet another hare-brained scheme which would probably end up in him making another hare-brained movie which, when it was finished, would probably leave them with less money in the bank than there was before the picture started.

Hetty Hurtzburger sighed again as she rubbed expensive vanishing cream into face wrinkles which simply refused to vanish no matter how hard and how often she rubbed. Life, she told herself again, was nothing if not extremely frustrating . . .

Life, Count Alucard told himself as he looked around the confines of the lifeboat, could be a whole lot worse. He had discovered a compartment which contained several lifebelts. These, when scattered about on the bottom of the lifeboat, would serve him as a comfortable bed. Better still, he had also discovered that the compartment held both a torch and a box of emergency rations. He had not yet opened the box but, by the light of the torch, he had read on the lid that the contents included tins of biscuits; cheese; soups; spreads and other nourishing items. More than sufficient to sustain him for several days, should he decide to remain in his hiding-place on the ship.

As soon as things quietened down outside, the Count told himself, he would prepare a substantial meal before settling down for the night. But what he did not understand was why there were sounds of so much movement on board at such a late hour. Running footsteps and raised voices. Surely, he asked himself, it was well past the time when all passengers – and most of the crew – should be abed? And yet, if anything, the noises seemed to be getting louder.

Count Alucard could contain his curiosity no longer. He would have to take a peep outside to see what, exactly, was going on. Taking hold of a corner of the lifeboat's canvas canopy, he lifted it no more than a couple of centimetres and peered through the gap.

Just at that moment, a group of men ran past the lifeboat led by a red-faced military-looking chap who, for some strange reason, seemed to be waving a pepper-mill around above his head. The men that came after him and who seemed to consist of both passengers and sailors, all looked as if they too were angry about something, for they were also brandishing items in the air: brooms, sticks and metal bars.

Some of the them were waving long-handled croquet mallets which seemed, to the Count, most curious of all. For it was surely much too late for anyone to be arranging deck games on board the ship?

"This way, men!" cried the red-faced military-man, as he led the charge along the deck. "We'll search the forward gangways next!"

And scarcely had that group been swallowed up into the night when, to the Count's surprise, another lot appeared and from the opposite direction. This second group, also made up of male passengers, and crew-members, was led by a bearded man in a roll-neck pullover. They were all carrying pointed things of one sort or another. Some of them wielded sharpened staves while others brandished gleaming skewers which, the Count guessed, must have come from the ship's kitchens.

"This way, men!" cried the bearded man in the roll-neck pullover, his eyes glinting fiercely behind his spectacles. "We'll search the gangways aft!"

Attempting to puzzle out this new turn of events, Count Alucard arrived at the opinion that this second group must be organizing a late-night barbecue on deck and that the skewers were intended for the spearing of kebabs. But *do* they have outdoor barbecues on ships, he wondered? Surely not! Wouldn't the risk of fire at sea rule out such a possibility?

But as he pondered on the advisibility of lighting open fires on the decks of cruise ships, an even stranger sight hove into view. It was one which served to strengthen the probability of a late-night shipboard party. For, as he continued to peer

61

through the narrow gap between the canvas cover and the lifeboat, Count Alucard blinked with astonishment as a youngish man, wearing nothing but a Donald Duck decorated bath-towel, padded barefoot across the deck. He was carrying a large tray of sandwiches.

The ship's purser, on returning to his cabin in order to properly dress himself in uniform, had discovered to his horror that the door was locked. He realised that it must have slammed shut behind him when he had previously made his hasty exit from the shower. Captain Summerhouse would be hopping mad, Fairweather told himself, at the sight of his purser still clad in the bath-towel. All the same, he thought, it would be wiser to go back to the dining-room with the sandwiches rather than empty-handed.

Count Alucard, of course, knew nothing of this. Neither did he have long to contemplate the purser's strange choice of clothing – or lack of it. For Fairweather had scarcely moved off in the direction of the dining-room, when a voice hissed out from behind the Count, causing him to almost leap out of his skin.

"Hey, Dracula! Gotta minute?"

The Count wheeled round instantly. Whilst he had been crouched inside the lifeboat, peering out, someone had been standing on the other side of the lifeboat, peering in at him.

"My name is Alucard – Count Alucard," gulped the vegetarian vampire nobleman, his heart still fluttering at the shock of being discovered.

"Sure it is," said the man, who spoke with an

American accent and had the butt of a cigar sticking out of one corner of his mouth. "But 'Alucard' is 'Dracula' backwards, okay?"

"That may indeed well be the case," replied the Count who had, by now, recovered all of his dignity. "But it does not give you the right to spy on me."

"Say now, is that a fact?" chuckled the American. "Well, just listen who's talking! You were spying on everyone and everybody that came within spitting distance, buddy."

"Whatever I was doing, was no concern of yours."

"Maybe it is – and maybe not," replied the man, using one podgy hand to hold up the lifeboat's canvas cover while he rubbed the top of his bald head with the other. "But I sure as hell know that the captain would feel that it was *his* concern – if he should happen to find out that Dracula was stashed away in one of the lifeboats."

"The name, as I have already told you, is 'Alucard'!" The Count paused, bit his lip, nervously, and then continued: "Are you going to tell him?"

"That all depends," said Hurtzburger, with a mysterious smile.

"Depends on what?"

"On whether or not you and I can do a deal?"

"What sort of deal?"

"That remains to be seen," said the famous film producer, as mysteriously as before.

"*What* remains to be seen?" asked the Count, who was beginning to tire of his visitor's refusal to come to the point. "Look here, I don't know what it is you want – but don't you think it might be wiser if you were to climb in under this canvas? If anyone should chance to pass and see you talking to a lifeboat – well, don't you think that it might look just a teeny bit suspicious?"

"Climb *inside*? With *you*?" It was the film producer's turn to look a little nervous. "Thanks – but, no thanks!" he added and his bald head shone as he shook it in the moonlight. "Do you think I'm nuts, or something? I don't want your fangs nipping my neck."

"I have never, in all of my existence, sunk my fangs into anyone's neck!" snapped the Count, his voice trembling with anger. "That's not the way that I behave at all and I'll thank you to remember that!"

"No?"

"*No*! Certainly not!"

"It's easy for you to say that, mister – but I'd prefer to see some proof of it."

"You have my word," replied the Count, proudly, as he straightened his black bow tie. "The word of an Alucard."

Hiram P. Hurtzburger hesitated for a moment and then lifted the canvas cover higher. "I guess I'll have to settle for that then," he growled as he clambered in through the opening at the opposite end of the lifeboat to where the Count was perched. "But you keep right there and I'll stay here."

"If that is what you wish," replied the Count, coldly, as the two men sat and faced each other, by torchlight, from each end of the lifeboat. "Now, sir," he continued, "I would be grateful if you would tell me what it is exactly that you want from me?"

"Want from *you*?"

"Of course. I imagine, that by doing me the favour of not revealing the fact that I am on this ship to the captain—"

"My not telling the captain that you're here?" broke in the famous film producer. "Don't you know that he knows already?"

"He does?"

"I'll say he does! Why, there are whole gangs of guys roaming the ship right now, with mallets and stakes they want to drive way deep down into your heart, buddy!"

There was a silence then which was broken, at last, by a long, soft sigh from the Count. "I suppose I should have guessed," he murmured, sadly.

Things never change, thought the Count. Why should they? Wheresoever I wander, be it on land or be it at sea, there will be those that want to hunt me down . . .

"Listen, Dracky-baby, you're getting me all wrong," Hurtzburger's voice broke in on the Count's thoughts. The famous film producer ground the stub of his cigar into the planking underneath his feet and, at the same time, reached inside his pocket for a replacement. "I don't want anything from you – I'm the guy that's looking to do *you* a favour."

"You want to help me?" said the Count, slightly nonplussed.

"I certainly do." Hurtzburger paused and jabbed his cigar in Alucard's direction. "Alucard, my friend, I'm gonna make you famous!"

There were several seconds of silence while the puzzled vegetarian vampire digested these words. The silence ended as the Count began to giggle. The giggle turned into a chuckle and the chuckle became a laugh. Count Alucard strove hard to laugh as quietly as he could while, at the other end of the lifeboat, Hurtzburger wriggled on his seat, impatiently.

"Did I say something funny?" growled the famous film producer.

The Count nodded and managed, finally, to control his laughter. "I *am* famous," he said. "That's always been my problem in life. In fact, given the opportunity, I'd like to meet someone who could make me a little *less* famous, thank you very much."

Hurtzburger frowned. "I'm not just talking

notoriety here, buddy," he said. "I'm talking fame
and riches. I'm talking gilt and gingerbread. I'm
talking *lifestyles*!"

"And I'm afraid that I haven't got the faintest
idea of what it is that you *are* talking about," said
the Count.

"Excuse me, Count. In the excitement of meeting
you I plain forgot to introduce myself." Hurtzburger fished into an inside pocket, reached down
the lifeboat and handed something to the Count.
"My card," he said.

Count Alucard shone the beam of the torch on
the small piece of pasteboard which the famous film
producer had handed to him and read the words
printed on it:

HIRAM P. HURTZBURGER
Famous Film Producer

Movies Made to Frighten the Pants Off Everyone!	Scary Films Inc., Hollywood, USA.

"I am extremely pleased to have made your
acquaintance," said the Count, after studying the
card. "But I still don't know what it is that you
want of me?"

"You don't?"

"I'm afraid not?"

"Do I need to spell it out for you?" said the
film producer, chomping excitedly on the end of his

cigar. "Alucard, my friend, I'm going to make you into a movie star!"

"I beg your pardon?"

" 'DRACULA!' starring 'Dracula!' " The glowing tip of Hurtzburger's cigar danced in the dark as he imagined the picture's title in enormous letters on a towering billboard. "Say – can't you just see the lines stretching away, as far the eye can see, outside of every movie-house in every corner of the world?"

"Forgive me, Mr Hurtzburger, but are you saying that you desire me to become an actor?"

"Nuts to acting!" gabbled the famous film producer enthusiastically. "Who needs actors? Actors are two a dime! '*Dracula IS Dracula!*' That's what it's gonna say in great big letters across every billboard! I just want you to be yourself, Drac . . . say, you don't mind me calling you, Drac, I hope? You just call me Hiram. We sure should be good buddies, Dracky-baby, if we're gonna make millions of bucks together. Did I say 'millions'? Forget it! We're talking mega-millions here! *Dracula IS Dracula*! is gonna make both our fortunes! And not just from the movie, Drac! No sir! There's gonna be all the marketing: Dracula drinking-mugs; Dracula pencil-tops; Dracula key-rings; Dracula glove puppets; Dracula bedspreads—"

"No, no, NO!" the Count's voice rose in his attempts to stem the famous film producer's flow of words.

"Okay, Drac old pal," Hurtzburger continued with a shrug. "No sweat. No bedspreads. You're right – they were a bad idea. We wouldn't want to scare the smaller kiddies and have them wake up screaming—"

"*Please*, Mr Hurtzburger! This has got nothing to do with bedspreads!"

"No? It's not the glove puppets, is it? They could be one of our biggest sellers."

"It's nothing to do with glove puppets either."

"No? If it's a question of your contract, Drac old buddy mine, rest easy. A straight fifty-fifty split, you and me, right down the middle."

"There isn't going to be a contract, Mr Hurtz-burger."

"Hey, Dracky-baby! What's bugging you?"

"The plain truth of the matter, Mr Hurtzburger, is that I have no wish to join you in your motion picture venture. In fact, I must insist that you banish all thoughts of such a preposterous scheme from your mind."

There were several moments of silence then while Hiram P. Hurtzburger digested this last statement. Silence, that is, beneath the lifeboat's canvas cover.

Outside, on deck, there were sounds of returning footsteps accompanied by the murmur of many voices. The search-parties, it seemed, had increased in number and were drawing closer to the lifeboat as they narrowed down their hunt for the fugitive vampire.

Count Alucard switched off the torch, as a precaution against being discovered, and the two men continued their conversation with their silhouettes just visible to each other in the glimmer of moonlight which filtered in through the narrow gaps in the canvas.

"Hey, c'mon now, Drac!" murmured Hurtzburger in tones of absolute disbelief. "Are you telling me that you don't *want* to be a movie star?"

In the half-dark under the lifeboat's cover, the famous film director could just make out the nod of the Transylvanian vampire Count's head. The footsteps were drawing even closer. The buzz of voices even louder. The same angry buzz, the Count reminded himself, that he had heard on several occasions – the last time it had come from the lane outside old Mrs Prendergast's cottage. Like the sound from a storm of angry hornets.

"There have been too many Dracula films already," said the Count, softly. "Far too many. It is time that the Dracula legends were forgotten. My forebears paid with their lives for their misdeeds. I would like to be left to live my life in peace. It is all I ask . . ."

The search-parties were close enough by now for the occasional loud cry to be heard above the growing murmur.

"I'll hold the stake over the blackguard's heart, while the rest of you hold him down!" shouted one excited voice. "I know exactly where to find the heart – I went to first aid classes!"

"And I'll drive home the stake with this heavy mallet!" roared a second voice. "Leave it to me, lads! I'll finish him with one almighty blow – I used to be a blacksmith!"

Inside the lifeboat, Hiram P. Hurtzburger gave a little shiver on hearing these bloodthirsty cries. He wondered, rather uneasily, what the Count was thinking – for there could be no doubt that the vegetarian vampire must have heard them too.

As if to confirm that fact, the shadowy figure sitting at the other end of the lifeboat suddenly rose to his feet. Standing tall and erect, his head brushing the highest part of the canvas awning, Count Alucard flung out his long, thin arms widespread, his hands gripping the edges of his black, voluminous cloak. The famous film producer cowered back, partly in surprise and partly fearing that he might be the one to suffer the full force of the vampire's outrage at his treatment by mankind.

Thankfully, Hurtzburger discovered, this was not to be the case.

"Farewell, Hiram P. Hurtzburger!" said the Count, the black silhouette of his outstretched cloak looming over the famous film producer. "I'm sorry that I could not see my way to assisting you in your cinematic endeavours – I feel sure though that they will be best forgotten. *Bon voyage!*"

Then, as Hurtzburger watched incredulously, the large black mass looming over him seemed suddenly to shrivel up in front of his eyes. He was then aware, but only for a moment, of the flutter of the same winged creature he had glimpsed, some hours before, outside the porthole of his cabin – the selfsame creature of the night, in fact, which had heralded the start of the curious chain of events. Another moment later, and the famous film producer snatched his last, brief glimpse of the vegetarian vampire bat as it squeezed its furry body out through the narrow gap between the canvas covering and the lifeboat – and then disappeared from sight.

Left alone in the lifeboat, with only his thoughts

71

for company, Hiram P. Hurtzburger pondered long and hard on what might have been. Sadly, he contemplated on how the opportunity of a film producer's lifetime had somehow slipped him by. "Cheer up!" said a small but optimistic voice inside his head. "There will be other opportunities!" But another voice that kept the first one company, spoke louder and with more conviction, telling him that lifetime opportunities presented themselves but once . . .

Hiram P. Hurtzburger let out a long, slow sigh then, deciding that what was past was best forgotten, put out a hand and lifted up the canvas awning. Putting his head outside the lifeboat, he was somewhat flustered to see a mass of angry faces staring back at him. He also noted that there were lots of hands, held aloft and waving mallets, hammers and suchlike implements, while others brandished stakes or skewers or other sharp-pointed things.

The two separate groups of vampire hunters had now combined and had just arrived outside the lifeboat intent on searching it from prow to stern.

"Hey! Go easy now!" gulped Hiram P. Hurtzburger as the milling men waved their weapons at him. "I'm not Dracula – I'm just another passenger on this ship!"

"Stand easy, men!" cried the red-faced military-looking man who was in the forefront of the party. Then, turning back to the famous film producer, he continued: "You haven't made contact with the quarry, I don't suppose? There isn't a tall, dark, sinister two-fanged chappie hiding inside that lifeboat?"

"Nope," replied the famous film director, a trifle sadly. "I haven't set eyes on a living soul."

"We're wasting our time here, men!" shouted the bearded man in a roll-neck pullover, his eyes glinting wildly behind his spectacles. "Let's go and search the engine-room."

Hiram P. Hurtzburger watched the gang of vampire hunters rush across the deck then, when the clatter of their urgent footsteps had faded down some distant stairway, he clambered out of the lifeboat and strolled off, dejectedly, towards his cabin.

Hanging upside down from the deck rail, hidden from sight by the lifeboat's hull, the beady-eyed, sleek-furred, snub-nosed vegetarian vampire bat eased its claws, one by one, from the woodwork. Spreading wide its black, parchment-like wings, the creature launched itself into the night. Heading into the chill wind that was coming off the Atlantic, the bat soared upwards into a sky pinpricked with glittering stars.

5

> *"This Old Man,*
> *He played one,*
> *He played knick-knack on my drum,*
> *Singing knick-knack paddy-wack,*
> *Give the dog a bone,*
> *This Old Man came rolling home . . ."*

After he had given out the cheese and tomato sandwiches, Nigel Fairweather, still dressed in nothing but the Donald Duck bath-towel, had been detailed by the captain to arrange some sort of communal activity in the ship's dining-room, in order to keep up the passengers' morale. Keen to accept the challenge – and eager, too, to get himself into the captain's good books for a change – the purser had begun by organizing a singsong for the younger children. When the chorus of the first song chosen echoed around the room, no one sang louder than Fairweather himself, as he led the singing from the platform, beating time with his loofah:

> *"This Old Man,*
> *He played two,*
> *He played knick-knack on my shoe . . ."*

Spiralling upwards on the sea breeze, the sound of the children's voices rose from the cruise ship into the moonlit sky where Count Alucard, in his bat form, swooped, then dived, then hovered as he flew steadily onwards into the oncoming wind. But as the *Orvatelle* sailed on towards the open sea, the black-winged creature fell behind and the winking lights of the cruise ship were swallowed up in the darkness while the sounds of the children's singing drifted into nothingness on the night air.

But Count Alucard was not sorry to see the cruise ship disappearing into the darkness. On the contrary, his short spell on the *Orvatelle* had provided him with nothing but problems. Neither was he sad at finding himself alone and flying above an empty starlit sea.

As for being lonely, Count Alucard had grown accustomed to leading a solitary life from early childhood. During his first schooldays, he had seemed to get along well with the other children until they learned of his identity – as soon as they discovered he was a Dracula, they tended to drift away and leave him to his own devices in a corner of the schoolyard. Over the years, he had managed to come to terms with loneliness and, indeed, had even grown to enjoy the solitary life.

With regard to his present predicament, in his bat form he not only understood but was also quite at home in the night-sky. Provided he could see the stars, then he would never get lost. Besides, he knew that he was flying above the Atlantic's shipping lanes and that, before very long, another vessel would come along affording him another lift towards his journey's end.

True enough, even as he pondered on his situation, his sharp bat's eyes picked out the lights of a large tanker which was heading out of the English Channel and going in the same direction as himself.

Count Alucard hovered for some seconds on his fine, dark outstretched wings and then turned and swooped towards the approaching vessel. This time, he decided, after he had found himself a warm and comfortable place to hide, he would think twice before letting himself be seen on deck.

The myriad twinkling lights of Manhattan by night were no less impressive, seen upside-down, as they would have been viewed right-side up. From his dizzily-high position, with his claws gripping tight on the elaborate stonework of the upheld torch of the Statue of Liberty, Count Alucard was hanging down and gazing across New York Bay towards the silhouetted skyscrapers of the city which lay beyond.

The journey across the Atlantic had taken the Count the best part of a week. He had flown during the night-time hours and rested, by day, on several ocean-going vessels that had chanced to come his way.

When, at last, he had first glimpsed the floodlit figure of the Statue – waiting to welcome him as she had welcomed so many previous visitors to the USA – the Count had resolved, there and then, to spend his first day's sleep in that country on the Statue itself. He had succeeded in finding a shadowy niche, out of the glare of the floodlighting beneath and, after taking in the Manhattan skyline, the vegetarian

vampire bat had enveloped his furry body with his parchment-like wings and allowed his tired eyelids to droop over his beady, jet-black eyes.

Not long after, the Statue of Liberty's floodlighting was switched off as the first fingers of a rosy dawn crept over the Bay. An early morning ferry, out of New York's Battery Harbour and headed for Staten Island, made good progress past the Liberty Statue. Over on the mainland the mighty, sprawling city, in company with its eighteen million inhabitants, was waking to the hurly-burly of yet another noisy, traffic-jammed, taxi-honking, vibrant New York day.

But Count Alucard, weary from his week-long ocean-spanning journey, was quite unaware of the sound and the colour and the urgency of the city coming to life – for he, himself, was fast asleep.

The Count slept soundly all through that day, hanging in his cosy niche on the rim of the torch and quite unnoticed by the many tourists who made the trip, by the speeding lift, up to the viewing platform in the Statue's head. When evening fell though, he was quick to wake, shifting his claws' grip on the stonework and enjoying again his curious downside-up bat's view of Manhattan.

But not for long. It was time for him to be on his way.

New York, he knew, was an exciting place – and it would have been exciting, too, to have spent a week or even longer, delighting in all that the city had to offer: Broadway shows and cinemas; hamburger-joints and hot dog stands; pizza and popcorn; posh art galleries and grand museums; Chinatown and Greenwich Village. But the bright lights and the hubbub of New York, he also knew, could not provide a hiding-place for a Transylvanian vampire Count, not even one that was a dedicated vegetarian.

No, the place for him, the Count had already decided, was to be found somewhere in the Midwest of America. In Indiana, perhaps, or Illinois, or Iowa, Wisconsin or Nebraska. A smalltown community of country folk who took a pride in keeping themselves to themselves and respected the privacy of others. He had thought that he had found exactly such a place, back in England, in his cosy little room in dear Mrs Prendergast's honeysuckle-scented cottage. If only that postman fellow could have had the decency to have minded his own business . . .

But this was not the time for looking back. Tomorrow was another day and the entire awesome length and breadth of the United States of America was his to explore.

Count Alucard slowly unfolded his dark, membraneous wings and gently loosed his bat's claw hold on the stonework of the torch held high by the Statue of Liberty. Then, after taking a deep breath, he launched himself onto the cool wind coming in from the Atlantic. He set off, with slow but steady wingbeats, over the Bay of New York, heading inland, westwards.

"Well now, honey," said the pretty black waitress, her neatly sharpened pencil hovering over her order-pad. "Have you made up your mind yet?"

"A thousand apologies, dear lady," murmured Count Alucard, gazing gravely across the counter of the otherwise empty diner at the many mouth-watering delicacies on the other side. "I'm afraid that I'm finding it awfully difficult to decide what it is I want."

"That's okay, honey, you take your time," replied the obliging lady, jabbing her pencil back into its usual resting place in her black mass of curls. "When you want me, you just sing out."

As the waitress drifted off towards the kitchen, the Count paused in his admiration of the good things on offer behind the counter and carefully picked off a strand of white cotton which had somehow attached itself to the sleeve of his otherwise impeccably neat black jacket. Count Alucard was, as always, concerned about his appearance. All things considered though, he complimented himself, he looked remarkably dapper for someone who had been on the move now for several months.

Not that he had been travelling without pause. There had been no need for that. America was a continent which he had never visited before and he intended to see all there was to be seen. He had taken his time, sometimes travelling by day, in human form, and sometimes on bat's wings and in the hours of darkness.

Through the lush Pennsylvanian farmlands first; then next across Ohio where he had paused for several days, in Cincinatti, and where his distinctive mode of dress had enabled him to find temporary employment as a nightclub doorman. Moving onwards, he had passed through Indiana; then Illinois; then on into Missouri where he had again broken his journey, when his musical skills had

80

made it possible for him to take a temporary post as a saxophonist in a St Louis jazz-band.

Finally, he had moved on into Kansas, the Sun-flower State and the very heartland of the Midwest – where Dorothy, in *The Wizard of Oz*, had been swept away by a 'twister' wind and off on her remarkable journey over the rainbow. There was something about the vast and seemingly endless fields of waving golden wheat that appealed to the vegetarian vampire Count. Perhaps here was the place where he might settle down?

"Yes, I might very well plump for that," murmured the Count aloud, as he perched on a swivel stool at the counter of the roadside diner, on the outskirts of a small Midwestern town called Double Springs.

"What's that?" asked the waitress, who had reappeared from the kitchen. "Have you made your mind up, honey?"

"Forgive me, dear lady," said the Count, with an apologetic shake of his head. "I was talking to myself. But I wonder if I might beg a favour of you? Would you mind, very much, explaining to me what all those good things are?"

"That's what I'm here for," replied that lady with a beaming smile as she, too, contemplated the row of delicious-looking pies and cakes and pastries on the glass display shelves. "Let me see now, we have Blueberry Pie; we have Apple Pie; we have Lemon-Meringue Pie; we have Pecan Pie; we have Chocolate-Cheesecake Pie; we have Boston Banana-Cream Pie – and if you're not in the mood for pie, we have Cranberry Upside-Down Cake, Lemon

Coconut Layer Cake; oatmeal cookies; Snickerdoodles, and a whole glass jar full of jelly doughnuts. So what's it going to be, honey? Which one of those is going to tickle your fancy?"

Count Alucard took a very deep breath and thought hard. It was, perhaps, the bat in him that made him settle, finally, on the Upside-Down Cake, which he washed down with a glass of frothy ice-cold milk.

An hour later, fully refreshed, the Count was striding out again on a long, straight and empty road which was bordered on both sides by seemingly endless fields of ripening corn. The sky was blue and clear and the air was heavy with birdsong. Count Alucard munched on an oatmeal cookie as he went along. Nothing, he told himself cheerfully, was wrong with his world. Had he thought a little harder, he might have reflected to himself that it was just at such times, when all seemed right, that Dame Fortune usually took it into her head to cruelly pull the rug from under his highly polished black patent leather shod feet . . .

Back in the diner, the pretty waitress frowned as she considered the question which had been put to her by the fatter of the two uniformed men who were sitting up at the counter, dunking doughnuts in their black coffee.

"Why, no, Sheriff," she said, shaking her head. "I can't say I've served any suspicious characters today, no way."

"Are you sure, Kitty?" growled Sheriff Wayne Tucker, wriggling his ample behind on the red plastic-covered seat of the stool which swivelled on its single chromium-plated leg. "We got a message on the car radio that a couple of bank robbers are high-tailing it in this direction. We sure as hell aim to catch 'em. Ain't that so, Brad?"

"It sure is, Sheriff. We sure as hell do!" agreed Deputy Sheriff Bradford Crick, his eyes gleaming behind his sun-glasses as he mumbled through a mouthful of coffee-soaked doughnut.

"There haven't been any bank robbers in this here diner Sheriff," replied the waitress, firmly, wiping down the countertop with a dishcloth. "Truth is, I haven't set eyes on any strangers since we opened this morning . . ." She paused and smiled as she remembered something and then continued: ". . . except for the funny tall, thin guy wearing the tuxedo who called in around two o'clock . . ."

"A tuxedo?" repeated the sheriff, frowning. "Are you telling me there was some kind of nut who was wearing a dinner jacket in the middle of the afternoon?"

"Yeah, but he wasn't no kind of a nut, Sheriff," replied the waitress, Kitty. "He was a nice kind of a guy. Very polite. He had better manners than most of the folk that live around these parts. He had two slices of Cranberry Upside-Down Cake, a glass of milk, and he went away with a quarter-pound of oatmeal cookies."

"What else was he wearing?" asked the sheriff, wiping the crumbs from his mouth with a paper napkin while, with his other hand, he proffered the waitress a five-dollar bill.

"Let me see now," said Kitty, as she placed the note inside the till and sorted out the sheriff's change. "He had on a stiff white shirt, a black bow tie, black trousers, shiny black shoes, there was a gold medallion round his neck on a chain and – oh, yeah! – he was carrying a black cape with a crimson lining."

"Sure as hell sounds like some kinda nut to me," repeated the sheriff. "What do you say, Brad?"

"Sure as hell sounds like some kinda nut to me too, Wayne," replied the deputy who, it should be stated, was given to agreeing, parrot-fashion, with everything his superior officer said.

"But he doesn't fit the description of either of the bank robbers," said Sheriff Tucker, a little sadly, "so you be sure and keep a weather eye open, Kitty, for any more strangers that stop by here."

"I surely will, Sheriff," said the waitress, putting the policeman's change in a saucer on the counter. "There you go now. Have a nice day!"

"I'll see iffen I can do just that, Kitty," said Sheriff Tucker, heaving his heavy frame off the stool and onto the well-scrubbed red-tiled floor. At the same time, he put out a hand to take up the money from out of the saucer. "Let's go, Brad! We'll drive along the North Fork Road and see if we can't—" The sheriff broke off as he held up one of the notes. "Hey, Kitty! What are you trying to do to me? This here ain't no dollar bill! This here's foreign currency."

"Let me see that," said the waitress, taking back the note. "Well, I'll be . . . you're right, Sheriff. It *is* a foreign bill. Now, just where in the name of heaven did I get that from?" As she spoke, Kitty turned the money over in her hand. At first glance, it did look very much like an American dollar. Whoever it was that had handed her the note in the first place, might very well have made the same mistake himself . . . "Hey!" continued the waitress. "I know! I guess I must have been given it by the funny guy in the tuxedo. Come to think of it, he did have a strange sort of acccent. He gave me two one-dollar bills – and I gave him some change. This must have got mixed in with those – but I'm sure it was an accident, Sheriff. He wouldn't have given me foreign money on purpose – he was the nicest, most well-mannered guy you ever saw."

"Let me see that bill again," growled the sheriff, unimpressed by Kitty's favourable description of her customer. Taking the foreign note from out of her hand he studied the lettering on it closely, then whistled softly to himself. "Nice and well-mannered was he, Kitty? You sure can count yourself lucky. You sure as hell had the narrowest escape of your life this afternoon." Then, turning to his deputy, he continued: "This here's Transylvanian money, Brad!"

"Transylvanian money?" repeated the deputy, blankly. "Well, waddaya know!"

"And just let's consider that location with the way the dude was dressed," continued the sheriff. "Black tuxedo, stiff white shirt, gold medallion, black bow tie, black trousers, shiny patent leather shoes and a flowing black crimson-lined cloak. Put those all together, Brad, and think 'Transylvania' and what do you have?"

"I swear I can't imagine, Sheriff Tucker," admitted the deputy, his eyes still blank behind his

sun-glasses. "What *do* you have?"

"Gosh darn it, Bradford Crick! Do I have to spell out everything for you?" Then, turning back to the waitress, he went on: "I'll ask you just one more question, Kitty – did the weirdo have two pointy teeth? Both in the upper jaw and one on either side of his mouth?"

86

"Why, Sheriff Tucker! He surely did! Now, how in the hoot did you know that?"

"By putting two and two together," replied the sheriff, with a modest shrug. "We can forget those bank robbers, Brad," he continued, turning back to his deputy. "We've got a far more serious problem on our hands. Seems like there's a goddarn blood-drinking vampire rampaging round the county."

"A blood-drinking vampire?" echoed the deputy with a little shudder. "Wow-eee!"

"A vampire?" repeated the puzzled waitress, open-mouthed. "You're not suggesting, Sheriff, that that nice, well-mannered gentleman—"

"I'm not *suggesting* anything, Kitty," snapped the sheriff, cutting her short. "I'm *telling*! Transylvania and pointy teeth and black tuxedos and cloaks with crimson linings spell vampires for certain sure – and if you'll take my advice, when Brad and me are gone, you'll lock the door of this diner, tight, and you won't open up again until I get on the phone and give you the say-so. C'mon, Brad, let's you and me go get us a vampire before the ornery crittur sinks his pointy teeth into some poor unsuspecting citizen of this here town."

With which, and without giving Kitty a chance to reply, Sheriff Tucker, with Deputy Sheriff Crick on his heel, strode out through the door of the diner, towards their waiting car.

"A *vampire*?" murmured the pretty waitress to herself. "He certainly didn't seem like no vampire to me. No, *sir*! No *way*!"

All the same, she took the sheriff's advice and crossed to put the "Closed" sign in the window. As the waitress slid home the bolts that secured the diner's door, both top and bottom, she heard the rise and fall of the police-car's wailing siren as the two law officers sped off along the long, straight Kansas country road, in pursuit of the wrongdoer.

Count Alucard's reputation, it seemed, had once again gone before him – even though it was completely without foundation.

6

Count Alucard's thin shoulders drooped as he sat on his hard, wooden bunk and gazed out glumly through the bars of his cell into the jailhouse corridor. Behind his head, through the small barred window high up on the dull green-painted wall, the evening sun was slowly dipping behind the red slate roof-tops of Double Springs.

But the vegetarian vampire had no intention of turning round to enjoy the last lingering moments of the red-gold sunset. What had started out as a pleasant day had turned into a thoroughly depressing one and the quicker that day turned into night, the Count told himself, the better. Casting his mind back, he considered the afternoon's dismal chain of events.

He had been leaning on a white-painted fence, sharing his last oatmeal cookie with a friendly pony, when the police car, containing Sheriff Tucker and Deputy Crick, had pulled up behind him with a squeal of brakes and in a cloud of dust. Scarcely aware of what was happening, he had felt himself being bundled, roughly, into the back of the police car, his slim pale wrists encased in a pair of shiny, nickel-plated handcuffs.

"There you go and there you stay, you ornery crittur," Sheriff Tucker had snapped as he had thrust his prisoner into the cell and slammed home the barred cell door. "Folks round these parts don't take kindly to having blood-drinking vampires dropping into this here county!"

"But I'm not a blood-drinking vampire—" the Count had started to protest. But it was no use. The sheriff had already gone and, moments later, the door to the office at the end of the corridor slammed shut behind him.

Count Alucard sighed, softly, as he pondered over his predicament. "They might at least have taken those off," he murmured as he glanced down at his hands which were still held securely and uncomfortably by the tight steel handcuffs.

Taking stock of his surroundings, he saw that the cells on either side of him were empty, as were those on the opposite side of the corridor. It seemed that he was to be denied companionship yet again. For the sake of passing the time, he lifted his manacled hands, felt inside his jacket pocket and lifted out the creased copy of the magazine, *The Coffin-Maker's Journal*, which he had placed there before hastily vacating his cosy room in old Mrs Prendergast's cottage some fourteen or fifteen weeks before.

"Is that all that it has been – just a few months?" the Count murmured to himself in some surprise. "Why, it seems almost like a lifetime ago! If only none of those events had taken place and I was back at that dear lady's now – reclining in a deckchair in her garden, perhaps, smelling the honeysuckle, listening to the evening bees and sipping at a glassful of her delicious rhubarb wine!"

But the Count was not the kind of man to mope for very long and, in spite of his surroundings, he soon forgot his problems as he lost himself in the contents of his favourite magazine. He had just turned to the centre-fold which contained a coloured illustration of a *de luxe* casket, fashioned out of ebony and with its interior white satin decorated with French embroidery, when he caught sight of a small, oblong piece of pasteboard which had slipped out of the pages of the magazine and fallen onto the stone floor. The Count leaned down, picked up the business card and reminded himself of what was written there:

And, as he stared at the card which the film producer had given him, while they had been sitting
under the canvas awning of the cruise ship's lifeboat,
an idea began to formulate in Count Alucard's
mind . . .

"Hey, Dracula! You've got a visitor." The voice
of Sheriff Wayne Tucker broke in on the vegetarian
vampire's thoughts.

"A visitor? For *me*?" said the Count, in some
surprise, hastily returning both the magazine and
the business card to his inside pocket. "But I don't
know a living soul in these parts!"

"I sure as hell bet you know a few dead ones
though!" chuckled the sheriff, darkly, and then,
when the Count disdained to react to his sombre
joke, continued: "This little lady says she knows
you – though why she would want to admit to that
fact, sure doggone beats me!"

"Who is it?" asked the Count, peering along the
corridor and into the darkness beyond. The evening
light was fading fast and it would soon be night.

"It's me," said Kitty, the pretty waitress from
the roadside diner, stepping out from the shadows.
She was carrying in both hands a small dish which

was covered with a clean, crisply ironed red and white check tea towel.

"My dear, dear lady!" cried the Count, puzzled but pleased by the waitress's appearance. "Whatever brings you to this sorry venue?"

The waitress shrugged, said nothing, but looked instead at the sheriff, hoping that she might be allowed a little time alone with the prisoner.

"Well, I guess that'll be okay, Kitty," growled the law officer, sensing what was in the young woman's mind. "But *only* a few minutes mind – and you'll have to talk to the dude through the bars. I wouldn't open that cell door not for all the hot dogs in Kansas – not even if they were smothered in onions and dripping with ketchup." With which, the sheriff turned and went off the way that he had come.

Kitty, still saying nothing, shuffled from one white-sneakered foot to the other, not knowing what to say. Now that she was alone with the Count, she was suffering a sudden attack of nerves.

"You still haven't told me why you've come?" said the Count, looking at his visitor encouragingly, through the bars.

The waitress blinked and chewed her lower lip. "The sheriff says that you're a vampire," she said at last. "And that you go round biting folk on the neck and drinking all their blood. Folk are saying the same thing too, all over town."

"But you don't believe them, do you?"

"Who says I don't?"

"You'd hardly be here now, alone with me, if you thought that it was true," replied the Count, a faint smile hovering on his lips.

"Truth to tell, I don't know *what* to think exactly!" said the waitress, tossing her head. "I *did* believe the sheriff in the diner. Then, after they had gone, I got to thinking – if you *were* a vampire, why hadn't you bitten *my* neck when we were alone together? You certainly had the opportunity. Then, when the news spread round the town that you'd been captured, I decided to come over to the jail and find out just exactly *what* you were myself."

"It was very good of you to come, dear lady. It was also extremely brave."

"Nothing of the kind," said Kitty, smiling at him through the bars of the cell. "I never did hear tell of a vampire that was partial to oatmeal cookies and Cranberry Upside-Down Cake . . ." She paused, gave a little frown, and then added, nervously: "You're *not* a vampire, are you?"

"Firstly, let me assure you that you have nothing whatsoever to fear, dear lady." The Count took a deep breath. He had decided to be nothing less than truthful with his visitor. "Having said that, I must admit that, when nightfall comes, I do have the ability to change into a bat."

"A *bat*?" said Kitty, with a gulp. "My sainted stars!"

"A *fruit*-eating bat," the Count continued, hastily. "My name is Alucard – Count Alucard. My father was a vampire count. So was my grandfather. I'm afraid that I am the odd one out in the family. I was born a vegetarian."

"Maybe I did the right thing for once then," said the waitress and, as he spoke, she lifted off the tea towel from the dish to reveal what was underneath.

94

"I'm afraid we were right out of the Cranberry Upside-Down Cake, so I brought along a slice of Blueberry Pie instead."

Count Alucard blinked back a tear. He was quite overcome with emotion and totally lost for words. It had been a long time since anyone had treated him with such kindness. He took his handkerchief out of a trouser pocket and blew his nose, hard.

"Now, you be sure and eat up every crumb of that," said Kitty, pushing the dish under the cell-door bars as she spoke.

"Thank you," said the Count.

The waitress watched as the Count picked up the dish with both of his manacled hands and then sank his pointy teeth through the inviting pastry-crust and into the juicy purplish-blue fruit. "Blood-drinking vampire my eye!" she said to herself. "Why, I never heard tell of anything quite so ridiculous in my entire life!"

A single overhead naked lamp came on, automatically, in the cell while the shadows lengthened in the corridor. It had grown quite dark outside. There was the sound of a door opening and then Sheriff Tucker's voice called out "Time to go, Kitty!"

"I shan't be more than a moment, Sheriff," the waitress called back. "I'm just saying 'goodnight'!"

"I'd make that 'goodbye', if I were you. They're coming to take him to the State Prison tomorrow morning. The way I see it, they're gonna find somewhere safe to put him – he ain't never gonna see daylight again. Not nohow. Just you be sure and make that 'goodbye' quick now!"

Inside the cell, Count Alucard did not seem at all

dismayed by the sheriff's words. Having finished the Blueberry Pie, he had taken his handkerchief out of his pocket, once again – this time to wipe the blueberry juice stains from the corners of his mouth.

"That was exceedingly delicious," said the Count, contentedly.

"Didn't you hear what the sheriff said, honey?" asked Kitty, puzzled. "It don't seem to me like you have as much chance as a turkey does come Thanksgiving."

Count Alucard smiled again, shook his head, pushed the empty pie dish back under the bars and then rose to his feet. He looked up at the high, barred window and out beyond it at the many stars now twinkling brightly in the night-sky.

"You seem to forget, dear lady, that I have a trick left up my sleeve," said the Count. "After I am gone, I would suggest that you call out loudly and immediately for assistance. I would certainly not wish for it to be thought that you were in any way involved in my escape."

"*Escape?*" gasped the flabbergasted Kitty. "What do you mean 'escape'? You surely don't imagine that you're going anywhere? You haven't got the keys to those handcuffs and I certainly don't possess the key to the cell."

The smile still hovered on Count Alucard's face. He rose to his feet, grasped the edges of his cloak and drew them close around his slim, tall body.

"Goodbye, dear lady," said the Count. "If ever we should chance to meet again, I trust that it may prove my pleasure to be able, in some small way, to repay your kindness . . ."

It seemed at first, to Kitty, as if the Count had begun to shrink. The handcuffs slipped over his thin, pale wrists and fell with a clatter onto the stone floor of the cell. Then, as the Count grew even smaller, his body and his clothes appeared to merge. The entire metamorphosis, from man to bat, could not have lasted longer than a second for, by the time it took Kitty to utter a short gasp of wonder, Count Alucard had disappeared entirely and she was staring at a small, dark furry creature hovering inside the cell on outstretched wings.

"Well, for gosh sakes . . ." murmured Kitty.

The bat edged closer towards where she stood, on the other side of the bars of the cell and, for several moments, gazed out at the waitress. Its eyes were bright and black and piercing – but there was a warmth of friendliness that glowed from inside

97

them. Then, suddenly, with a quick beat of its wings, the creature turned and flew up to the window, slipped easily through the bars – and was gone.

"Why, I never saw the like of that in all of my existence," said Kitty, softly to herself. Then, remembering what the Count had said, she shouted, loudly: "Sheriff! Sheriff Tucker! Come quick! The prisoner's just got away!"

There was the sound, again, of a door being flung open and then light spilled out along the corridor. A moment later, Kitty was joined by Sheriff Tucker and his deputy, Bradford Crick. The two law officers stood gazing into the locked but empty cell, unable to believe their eyes.

"What in tarnation happened?" mumbled the sheriff, blinking in amazement. "Where did the goddarned evil crittur go, Kitty?"

"Yeah, Kitty?" gasped Deputy Sheriff Crick. "Where in tarnation did the ornery crittur get to?"

"Don't ask me, Sheriff," replied the pretty waitress, biting back a smile. "He just kinda disappeared. One minute he was sitting on that bunk, as large as life – all at once, he just wasn't there no more. He disappeared entirely right into thin air."

The two law officers turned and looked at each other, open-mouthed, and then they looked back into the empty cell.

"Well, I'll be hog-tied," muttered Sheriff Tucker.

"I'll be hog-tied too," said Deputy Sheriff Crick.

"What worries me the most, Brad," said the sheriff, "is what we're going to tell those state prison officers when they arrive tomorrow morning and the prisoner ain't here no more?"

"You know something, Sheriff?" replied the deputy. "That's what worries me most too. Exactly what we're gonna tell those state prison officers tomorrow morning when—"

"Bradford Crick!" snapped Sheriff Tucker, cutting his deputy short. "If you don't have anything new to say on the subject – apart from repeating what I've just said – then I certainly would appreciate it if you'd keep your mouth shut!"

With which, the sheriff turned his back on his deputy and stamped off towards the office.

"I don't see why he has to take it out on me," said Deputy Sheriff Bradford Crick, turning to the waitress. "Warn't no fault of mine that the prisoner got away, was it, Kitty?"

The waitress gave the deputy a sympathetic smile as she shook her head. Then, after he had walked off in the same direction as his superior officer, head bowed and feeling badly done by, Kitty turned to look across the empty cell and at the window high up on the wall. Beyond the bars, the stars shone bright as diamonds in the black velvet sky.

"Good luck, Count Alucard," whispered Kitty, addressing the night air. "I don't know what it is that you're looking for – but I certainly hope that you find it one day . . ."

And, so saying, she tucked the empty pie dish under her arm and moved off along the corridor towards the police-station's exit and the smalltown streets that lay beyond.

Beyond Kansas, the flat agricultural land of the

99

Midwest gave way to the mountain states. Count Alucard, in his bat form, flew ever onwards, night after night, over vast regions of peaks and canyons; across wide, silent rivers which shone silver in the moonlight; travelling steadily but surely towards the West Coast of America which fringed the great Pacific Ocean.

He did not dally longer than a single day in any territory, for he knew now not only where he was going, but what he intended to do there once he had arrived. There was a purpose to his travelling and he meant to reach his destination just as quickly as his strong, parchment-like wings would take him.

Across the mountains of Colorado first, then on through Utah, over the countless miles of national parks, then bordering the rim of the Grand Canyon, and on into Nevada. It was in Nevada that the Count did choose to stay for a while.

Well, why not? He had been travelling now for quite some time and it seemed, to him, a good idea to take a few days off before flying on, into California, and the last leg of his journey.

Also, he had found himself attracted by the bright lights of Las Vegas. The gambling city, sitting out in the bare Nevada Desert, proved an ideal spot in which to lose himself for a short while. His black cape seemed not at all out of place in the night-time world of Las Vegas's casinos; nightclubs; cabaret spots and lush hotels. Thus dressed, he was able to stroll through the city's broad streets at his leisure by night, without anyone giving him so much as a second glance.

He also managed to find himself some comfortable

daytime sleeping quarters: in the belfry of a wooden bell-tower which belonged to a tiny wedding-chapel. Each morning, as dawn moved into day, he would fold his bat's wings around his body and hang upside-down inside the belfry until evening fell and the colourful lights from the tall hotels and the entertainment centres summoned him again.

There were some days though when he did not sleep. For he soon discovered that his services as a witness were more than welcome at many of the weddings which took place in the chapel. Shy, young, eloping couples from the East, arriving in the city, were grateful to have his well-dressed good-mannered presence at their marriage ceremonies. Afterwards, they would invite the Count to join them at their wedding breakfast, where he would drink chilled champagne and feast on crispy lettuce; thick slices of juicy beef tomatoes; gruyere cheese on rye bread; and luscious Californian peaches.

They were brief friendships – but the Count enjoyed those happy moments with the newly-wed couples who, having eyes only for each other, did not ask questions of the curious stranger who had been able to oblige them at their wedding cere-monies.

But all good things, eventually, must end. The night fell when Count Alucard arrived at the opinion that he had rested long enough and that it was time for him to continue his journey.

Taking his last late evening stroll along the broad avenues of the city, he went in through the plate glass doors of the largest of the Las Vegas hotels. Once inside the swish foyer, he took a lift up to the topmost floor. From there, he found a flight of stairs which led out onto the deserted rooftop. Crossing to the edge, he gazed past the glittering city lights out into the gathering gloom beyond which lay the desert.

Then, clambering up onto the narrow parapet, he took hold of the edges of his cloak and spread his arms out wide.

"California, here I come!" cried Count Alucard, as he launched himself onto the warm night air of Nevada.

7

"Will you take a look at that, Miss!" breathed the white-aproned elderly waiter, fearfully, peering out of the seafront restaurant's window from his hiding-place beneath the table. "It's . . . it's a giant lobster! It must be eight foot long! And it's headed this way. Just look at those claws – why, I fancy it could take a man's head clean off his body with a single snap of either one of those!"

"Stay cool, Lucky!" responded the beautiful golden-haired girl who was crouched at the waiter's side – and who was wearing nothing but a bikini. "Whatever happens, don't move so much as a muscle. I don't think that it's spotted us yet. If we keep perfectly still, and don't make a sound, perhaps it will go back down the beach. That would give the marines a chance to tackle it."

But even as the girl was speaking, the giant-sized crustacean lifted one of its enormous claws and brought it down hard, on the window, smashing both glass and wooden framework into smithereens.

"Heaven preserve us, miss!" screamed the waiter, his eyes bulging with fear. "I think it's got us in its sights! It's coming straight towards us!"

"Get a grip on yourself, Lucky!" snapped the girl

in the bikini, taking a tight grip on the boathook she had previously lifted down from its resting place behind the bar. "The one thing we must *never* do, is let that awful creature realise that we're afraid of it!"

By now, the huge lobster had succeeded in shoving its ugly shell-armoured head in through the window. Its jet-black, beady eyes had swivelled and were glaring down at the old, trembling waiter and the spirited girl who were cowering underneath the table. Green clouds of smoke were billowing, angrily, from the creature's nostrils—

"Cut!" came the voice of the film director from the studio floor.

"Cut? *Cut!* Did you say 'Cut', Howie?" called the film's producer, shuffling his behind uneasily in the wood-and-canvas chair which bore his name in big white letters across its back: HIRAM P. HURTZ-BURGER. "Whaddaya wanna call 'Cut' for, Howie? I thought the scene was going just great." As he spoke, Hurtzburger chewed angrily on his stub of a cigar, shifting it from one corner of his mouth to the other.

On the set of the studio floor, the actor and actress playing the parts of 'ELDERLY WAITER' and 'GIRL-IN-A-BIKINI' had crawled out from underneath the restaurant table in order to stretch their legs.

"I'm sorry, Mr Hurtzburger," said Howard Frost, the young director. "I'm afraid I wasn't too happy with the lobster."

"Was it something I did wrong, Mr Frost?" asked the man inside the lobster costume, having already removed his lobster head and taken one hand out of a lobster claw in order to wipe the sweat from his brow with a Paisley-patterned handkerchief. "Would you like more smoke from out of the nostrils? Do you want for me to swivel the eyes a little faster?"

"No, no," replied the director, thoughtfully. "The swivelling eyes were fine – just fine. But, yes, Harvey, it was the smoke that bothered me—"

"What was wrong with the way he did the smoke?" snarled Hurtzburger. "I thought he did the smoke just great."

"Well, it wasn't the *way* he did the smoke, Mr

105

Hurtzburger," said Howard Frost, choosing his words carefully, not wanting to anger his producer. "I just wonder whether we really need the smoke at all?"

"What's wrong with the smoke?" snapped Hurtzburger, getting angry. Having green smoke come out of the lobster's nostrils had been his own idea.

"Well, now," began the director, nervously. "I wonder whether a *real* lobster would have green smoke coming out of its nostrils? They do live under the sea, after all. I'm not too sure that lobsters have got nostrils for smoke to come out of—"

"Have you ever seen a lobster that was eight feet long?" interrupted the producer.

"Well, no, I can't say that—"

"Then how would you know whether it could blow out green smoke or not?"

"Well—"

"Excuse me, Mr Frost," interrupted the GIRL-IN-THE-BIKINI. "But if we've broken, would it be okay if I went to Make-up? It's awfully dirty underneath that table – I seem to have got a smudge of dust or something on my chin."

"Very well, Sharon," said the director, with a sigh. "I want you back on the set in five minutes though."

"Excuse me, Mr Frost," said the ELDERLY WAITER. "May I go to Wardrobe? I have a tear in my apron that needs a couple of stitches – I think I snagged it on a nail under the table."

"Well, okay, Oscar, if you must," said the director, sighing again. "But just see that you make it snappy."

"Say, Mr Frost, sir!" called out the man in the lobster costume. "Would it be okay for me to go to the First Aid Room? The bottom half of this costume is awful tight – I've got cramps in my right leg real terrible!"

"Better let the nurse take a look at it then, Harvey," said Howard Frost, letting out yet another sigh. "Best not take any chances."

"Thanks, Mr Frost, sir."

The man in the lobster costume limped off slowly across the studio floor, carrying his lobster head in one hand and with the lobster claw he had taken off clamped tightly in the lobster claw he was still wearing.

Howard Frost watched the headless lobster go out through the soundproof door then, after glancing at his watch, he bowed to the inevitable and called out to the entire studio workforce: "I guess that's shooting finished for today, folks. But bright and early tomorrow morning, everybody! I want to start at 7.30 sharp. We'll begin with the scene where the lobster nips off Lucky's head."

The several camera-men switched off their cameras, the sound-men climbed down from their microphone-boom platforms and, as the electricians turned off the overhead floodlights, the studio set was plunged, instantly, from brilliance into half-gloom.

"Do you wanna know something, Howie," growled Hiram P. Hurtzburger when, moments later, the studio floor was empty apart from the young director and himself, "We've only been in production for a week and we're two days behind on shooting already."

107

"I did tell you, when I first read the script, that *Lobster Raiders* wouldn't be an easy movie to shoot, Mr Hurtzburger," replied the young director. "And so far we've only got the *one* lobster on the set. Wait until the studio's *crawling* with extras wearing those lobster costumes – and all of them blowing out green smoke at once – and then let's you and me talk about what is, or what isn't, difficult!"

The film director, having summoned up his courage and spoken his mind, walked out of the studio. The soundproof door swung shut behind him. Hiram P. Hurtzburger, left all alone, slumped down in the chair which had his name printed across its canvas back and considered his problems.

A couple of months before, when he had chosen *Lobster Raiders* from the pile of scripts on the bedside table of the cruise ship's cabin, he had known that he was having to settle for second-best. The movie which he had *really* wanted to make was the one which would have starred the real-life vampire count he had found hiding, under the canvas awning, in the *Orvatelle*'s lifeboat. All the same, *Lobster Raiders* had seemed a better bet than any of the other scripts which he had read. He had discarded *The Curse of the Carrot People* instantly. He had not wasted time in reading past page nine of *Sewer Rats In Outer Space*. He had not so much as bothered to turn the title-page of *The Cockroach That Conquered Earth* . . .

"That vampire movie sure would have been one helluvah movie," muttered the film producer to himself as he reached inside his pocket for a new cigar. He wondered where the vampire bat had headed for, when it had crawled out under the lifeboat's canvas and flown off into the starry night. "One thing's for sure," he continued musing to himself. "There's no way that Alucard guy is going to show his face in Hollywood – you've just gotta face facts, Hiram, you're never gonna set eyes on that vampire again—"

"Sorry to bother you, Mr Hurtzburger, sir . . ." It was Eddie, the studio's security guard. "I found this weirdo wandering round on the back lot. He says he's here to see you."

Hiram P. Hurtzburger turned his head and stared, scarcely able to believe his eyes, at the tall, pale man whose arm was held in a tight grip by the uniformed security guard. The man was wearing a black suit, a starched white shirt, and a black bow tie. A gold medallion hung on a gold chain around his neck. He also had a black crimson-lined cloak thrown over his shoulders.

"Good afternoon, Mr Hurtzburger," said Count Alucard holding up, in his free hand, the business card which the producer had handed to him, all those several months ago, in the *Orvatelle's* lifeboat. "I wonder if you remember meeting me?" Then, with a shy, apologetic smile, he added: "I trust that I am not inconveniencing you at all?"

"No way!" exclaimed Mr Hurtzburger, rising hurriedly to his feet. Then, flinging wide his arms, he strode across the studio floor to greet the Count. "It's okay, Eddie. Let go of him. Count Alucard is an old buddy of mine."

"Are you sure that you won't let me barbecue you

a hamburger, Drac?" said Hiram P. Hurtzburger, who was wearing a cook's striped apron and a chef's white hat. He was, as always, chewing on a cigar.

"No, thank you, Mr Hurtzburger," replied the Count. "It's exceedingly kind of you to offer but, no – a bowl of that delicious-looking green salad will more than suffice."

"Are you absolutely positive, Count Alucard, that I can't tempt you with just one teensy-weensy glass of wine?" asked Mrs Hurtzburger who, having dressed up for the occasion in her best black evening dress trimmed with gold, was hovering attentively over the Count's chair with a bottle in one hand and an empty glass in the other.

"Please don't take offence, dear lady," replied the Count. "But I would far, far rather – provided that you have no objection – sip at a glass of that fresh grape juice I seem to see over there."

They were out on the wide, multi-coloured patio of the Hurtzburgers' grand home in Beverly Hills, that most fashionable part of Los Angeles where only the rich and famous live. Hetty Hurtzburger, who was overjoyed to be entertaining a Translyvan-ian Count (once it had been made clear to her that their guest was harmless), was dispensing drinks from a glass-topped gold-plated table, while Hiram was preparing the evening meal on the nearby barbe-cue. Count Alucard meanwhile, was relaxing on the green and pink striped, soft upholstery of a luxur-ious reclining-chair which was positioned by the edge of the Hurtzburgers' floodlit private swimming pool.

110

As he gazed across the still, blue illuminated sur-
face of the water, the Count considered the last stage
of his awesome solo flight which had taken him right
across the United States from the East Coast to the
West.

Leaving Las Vegas behind, he had headed into
California, across the white sand wastes of Death
Valley, near the vast Mojave Desert, which is the
hottest, driest area in the entire USA. From there
he had been forced to urge his tired wings to their
very limits in order to rise up and soar over the
snow-covered peaks of Mount Whitney, then
onwards again, over more pleasant terrain and
towards the Pacific Ocean and Los Angeles.

Count Alucard pondered also on the decision he
had taken which had resulted in his flying that great
distance across the continent of America – a decision
that had been prompted by the small oblong piece
of pasteboard which the film producer had handed

to him in the bottom of the *Orvatelle's* lifeboat—

"Here's your grape juice, Count," simpered Hetty Hurtzburger, breaking in on his thoughts.

"You are most kind, dear lady," murmured Count Alucard, smiling up at his hostess. In the blue translucent light that came from out of the swimming pool, Hetty Hurtzburger's blue-rinsed hair, it seemed, had taken on an almost ghostly glow.

"And do you think that you might care to try a pre-dinner nibble, Count?" asked the film producer's wife, proffering a plate containing a selection of bite-size snacks.

"Your hospitality is indeed boundless," replied Count Alucard selecting, between forefinger and thumb, a dainty cracker heaped with blue cheese and surmounted by a sliver of olive stuffed with pimento. Munching on this titbit, he glanced across to where the famous film producer was busy at the barbecue and then returned to a conversation they had been having several minutes before: "If that most generous offer of an acting career, which you once made to me, Mr Hurtzburger, is still open, then I am of a mind to take you up on it."

"Is it ever!" announced the film producer, cheerfully. As he spoke, Hurtzburger slapped a heap of sliced onions onto the barbecue's hotplate where they spat and sizzled, noisily, beside some already grilling hamburgers. "If you wanna be a movie star, Drac old pal, then I'm the guy to make you one!"

"It is not so much a desire to achieve screen stardom," explained the Count, choosing his words carefully, "as a need to present my true persona to the widest possible audience."

"Dracky old buddy," replied the famous film producer and, as he spoke, he flipped over the hamburgers on the barbecue onto their uncooked sides, "between the two of us, we're gonna do exactly that."

"A film which will show me to the world in my very best light."

"You said it, Drac!" enthused Hurtzburger, turning the spitting onions at the same time. "We're really gonna go to town with this movie. Just wait until the make-up department goes to work on you: the pointy teeth; the deathlike pallor; the spooky red-rimmed eyes; the blood dripping down off the end of your chin . . . The hairy, scary bat that swoops down at full moon and gets its fangs into the heroine's smooth, white throat—"

"No, no, no, Mr Hurtzburger!" broke in the Count, waving his long, pale hands in the air in disapproval. "That's not the kind of film I have in mind at all. I want to *improve* my public image – not make it worse. That's the whole point. I want to make a film which shows me as I really am – a *caring* person. I would like to be the hero, not the villain. I did not fly all the way across America, believe me, in order to be portrayed as more of a monster than I really am. I'm sick and tired of being hated and despised wherever I go. I would like to be liked. I want to have *friends* . . ." The Count paused, gave both of the Hurtzburgers an embarrassed smile and then added, shyly: "I would like to be loved."

"But you *are* loved, Dracky-baby," replied the

113

famous film producer. "*I* love you. You're the best thing that ever happened to Scary Films Incorporated. C'mon, Drac, let's make the movie, you and me? Huh? Waddaya say?"

"Most certainly not."

"Okay, Drac. How about this for an idea? First of all, we make *Dracula* IS *Dracula*! the way I told it with the pointy teeth, the spooky bloodshot eyes, the dripping blood and the scary, hairy bat that goes around sinking its fangs into everybody it comes across, then – maybe next year, maybe the year after that – we get to make the sequel, *Dracula* IS *Dracula II*!, and then we let you be the good guy?"

"I'm sorry, Mr Hurtzburger," replied the Count, who had been shaking his head firmly all the time that the film producer had been speaking. "I'm afraid I must insist. Either you make the film the way that I say – or I cannot allow myself to be associated with it in any way."

"You certainly do drive a hard bargain, Drac old pal," said the famous film producer, lifting the hamburgers which were now cooked to a turn, off the barbecue and on to a plate. "But if that's the way you feel – okay. You win. We'll make the movie your way." Hiram P. Hurtzburger flashed the Count his biggest, broadest and most reassurring smile, and then added: "Are you sure that you won't try just one of these burgers, Dracky-baby? They're delicious."

"No, thank you, Mr Hurtzburger. I'm strictly a vegetarian. But I will help myself to some salad."

"Hiram Hurtzburger, have you *completely* flipped your lid?" hissed Hetty Hurtzburger heatedly at her

114

husband, the moment that the Count had turned towards the salad bowl. "You can't make a movie with a vampire as the good guy. You'll get yourself laughed out of Hollywood!"

"Leave it to me, Hetty," Hurtzburger whispered back. "Once I've got this guy's signature on a contract, we'll make the movie the way *I* decide. Meanwhile, we'll butter him up. If you want to move into that mansion up on the hill with the *two* swimming pools, be nice to the sucker, Hetty—" The famous film producer broke off as the Count turned back towards them, an ample helping of lettuce, avocado and chopped walnuts on his plate. "That's the idea, Drac old buddy," Hurtzburger continued. "Eat! Enjoy! And no more talk of movies tonight, eh? You just sit back and leave the business side of things to me."

"More grape juice, Count?" simpered Hetty Hurtzburger, giving the Transylvanian nobleman an even wider smile than the one her husband was wearing as she reached for the empty glass. "Do please allow me to give you a refill."

"You are too kind, dear lady," replied the Count, politely.

"Did I hear you right, Mr Hurtzburger?" gasped Howard Frost, the film director, who had arrived at the studio in the early hours of the morning, only to discover that the entire crew and all the actors had been sent back home. "Did you say that you are cancelling the movie?"

It was not yet light. The moon was still shining in the sky. The famous film producer and the young director were strolling in a walkway between two giant studios, both as big as aircraft hangars.

"Nope," growled Hurtzburger, puffing energetically on his first cigar of the day. "We're not pulling the plug on *Lobster Raiders* – we're gonna make some script changes that's all. Only it ain't gonna be called *Lobster Raiders* any longer – the new title is *Dracula IS Dracula*! – and just wait until you hear this one, Howie – we're getting us a real live vampire count to play the starring role. How about *that*?"

"But what about all the lobster costumes, Mr Hurtzburger?" protested the young director. "They cost an absolute fortune."

"They won't be wasted, Howie, don't you worry. We're keeping the giant lobsters in the new version – except that now the lobsters are the good guys."

"We're having eight-foot killer lobsters, breathing out green smoke, for good guys?" The young film director could scarcely believe his ears. "Wow!" he added softly.

"Sure, Howie," replied Hurtzburger, shifting his cigar around the corners of his mouth in his usual fashion. "The way I'm having the script rewritten, the lobsters get to save the world."

"From who?"

"Like I told you, Howie, from the evil, stary-eyed, pointy-toothed, blood-drinking, scary vampire, who else? Go home and pack your suitcase, and prepare to travel. We're gonna make the entire movie on location – in the Count's own country: Transylvania."

"Did you say with a *real* vampire?"

"Sure thing. This guy's certainly for real. Don't take my word for it – figure it out for yourself, Howie. His name's Count Alucard – that's Dracula spelled backwards."

"*Wow!*" murmured the young director for a second time. "And has he agreed to be in the picture?"

"He *wants* to be in the picture. He came to me. The picture was his idea. Would I lie to you, Howie?" Hurtzburger took the cigar out of his mouth and thoughtfully studied its glowing end in the darkness. "I'm gonna have to lie to him though, for the time being at least. Me and the Count don't quite see eye to eye on the *kinda* movie we're gonna make."

"What kind of movie is that, Mr Hurtzburger?"

"Like I told you, Howie, the horror movie to end all horror movies – until we make the sequel: *Dracula Conquers The Universe!*" The famous film producer returned the cigar to one corner of his mouth which had spread into a happy grin. "Believe me, Howie-baby, we're gonna make a fortune outta this crazy vampire guy! Think of the marketing: Dracula posters; Dracula bedspreads; Dracula key-rings—" He paused, thought hard, then punched a pudgy fist into the air as he continued: "Hey! How about this for a money-spinner? We'll market spooky Dracula dolls that the kids can pull the arms and legs off!"

"Would kids *want* to pull the arms and legs from off their dolls?" asked the film director with a puzzled frown.

The two men had arrived at the end of the long

walkway between the two massive studio buildings. It was beginning to get light. Across the valley, they could just make out the big white letters H-O-L-L-Y-W-O-O-D which were positioned high up, on the hills that rose up over the movie capital.

"Howie-baby, when Joe Public gets to see this movie, *everybody's* gonna want to pull the arms and legs from off this vampire guy. Moms, dads, kids – grannies even! We're gonna make a picture that makes Dracula the most hated being on the face of the earth. And you and me, Howie, we're gonna make *millions*. Mega-bucks."

Then, flushed with delight at the thought of the fortune that was within his grasp, Hiram P. Hurtz-burger reached inside his jacket for a new cele-bratory cigar.

As daylight dawned up on the hills above Los Ange-les, the vegetarian bat which was hanging upside-down beneath the upper curve in the second big letter "O" of HOLLYWOOD, loosed its claw-hold and fluttered gently to the grassy slope below. A moment later, it had transformed itself into a tall, slim black-suited angular figure wearing a crimson-lined cloak.

Count Alucard, who had slept well under the Californian night-sky in his bat form, felt inside his jacket pocket and carefully lifted out a folded paper-napkin. Inside the napkin were several slices of avocado he had saved for himself from his previous night's supper at the famous film producer's Beverly Hills home.

"Such charming people, the Hurtzburgers," the Count murmured to himself as he chewed on his avocado breakfast. "I'm really looking forward to starring in this movie."

But at that moment in time, of course, Count Alucard had no idea of the kind of movie in which Hiram P. Hurtzburger was planning for him to play the starring role.

8

"Holy cow! Where have you seen that face before, Brad?" asked Sheriff Wayne Tucker, pushing the open magazine, left behind by a previous customer, across the table.

"Can't rightly say, Sheriff," replied Deputy Sheriff Bradford Crick, peering at the photograph in the magazine. "Where have I seen that face before exactly?"

"A fine sort of deputy I chose for myself," snorted the sheriff. "Can't you pick out an escaped prisoner when his picture's right in front of your eyes? That's that gosh-darned vampire that broke out of jail 'bout four or five months ago."

"Why, so it is, Sheriff! That gosh-darned vampire! How come he's got his photie in a movie magazine?"

The two Kansas law officers, having spent most of the morning unsuccessfully pursuing a couple of car thieves, were taking a well-earned break for coffee and doughnuts in their favourite roadside diner.

"I'll tell you what he's doing, Brad, seeing as how you've asked – he's starring in a horror movie, that's what." As he spoke, the sheriff ran a forefinger down the words which accompanied the picture of Count Alucard. "Seems like the varmint high-tailed it all the way to Hollywood after he made that jail-break – and some dang fool movie producer has given him the leading part in this here film."

"You don't say, Sheriff! Now what kind of a dang fool movie producer would do a thing like that?" asked the Deputy Sheriff.

"Search me, Brad," replied Sheriff Tucker and, as he spoke, he ripped the page containing the photograph and the article that accompanied it out of the magazine. "But I sure as hell know this – that movie ain't never going to happen, not if I have anything to do with it." Then, rising to his feet, he added brusquely: "C'mon!"

"Where to, Sheriff?" gulped Crick, who had not yet finished either his coffee or his second doughnut, and was looking up at his superior officer in some surprise.

"Why – Transylvania, where else?"

"*Transylvania?*"

"You've said it, Brad! You an' me, Brad Crick, are gonna go out there and fetch that ornery crittur back so's he c'n stand trial, get found guilty, and then serve his sentence right and proper."

"But Sheriff Tucker," began the deputy with a gulp, "we're *Kansas* lawmen – we can't just high-tail it off to Transylvania when it takes our fancy. Transylvania must be . . . must be . . ." he paused, not knowing quite where – or how far away – that country was. ". . . Transylvania must be *thousands* of miles away from Kansas," he finally concluded.

"That's true, Brad," Sheriff Tucker agreed. "But

I'll tell you what I'm aiming for us to do. Now, I haven't taken any vacation so far this year – and I know for a certain fact that you ain't neither. So we're gonna go out there in our own time and arrest that nogood vampire."

"In our own time, Sheriff?" wailed Deputy Crick. "Why, I was planning on going to Disneyworld this year for my vacation – they've got a dandy brand new roller-coaster there I was intending to take a ride on and—"

"Bradford Crick!" snapped Sheriff Tucker. "That ornery vampire made a laughing stock of both of us when he broke jail the way he did – now, are you gonna get your good name back, with every lawman in this county, or are you gonna let that gosh-darned vampire get away with things?"

"No, Sheriff, but—"

"Okay – so let's you and me go and see the mayor right now and fix it so's we can get to go to Transylvania."

The sheriff's deputy sighed, clambered to his feet, drained his coffee-cup, slipped his last mouthful of doughnut into his mouth and followed his superior out of the diner. Moments later, when the sound of the police car's siren had faded into the distance, the door to the kitchen swung open and the waitress, Kitty, entered the restaurant. She looked around at the empty chairs and tables and shook her head in some dismay.

"It sure is a lonely life in a roadside diner without no customers to pass the time of day," she told herself wistfully.

Things were not going well at her place of employment. Business had been dropping off steadily since the opening of the new freeway – together with that freeway's own smart neon-lit hamburger-and-pizza-palace – several miles away. There were few cars these days that chose a route which led past the roadside diner. The long rows of glass display shelves, behind the counter, which had previously been piled high with cheesecakes, chocolate cakes and other good things too numerous to mention, were now almost empty. There was little point in stocking shelves without the customers to buy those goods. And, when the occasional passers-by did choose to drop into the diner, they usually took one glance at the empty shelves and walked straight out again.

"Maybe the time has come when you should start looking somewhere else for employment, Kitty," the waitress murmured sadly to herself. She wondered why the sheriff and his deputy had left in such a hurry – without even staying long enough for her to give them her usual cheery: "Have a nice day!" Kitty sighed again as she cleared the used coffee-cups and the other debris from off the table where the two law officers had recently been sitting. "Working in a diner without anyone to talk to is dull and plain downright *boring*!" she concluded softly.

Coincidentally, it was at that selfsame moment that Kitty's eyes chanced to fall on the open movie magazine which the sheriff had left behind. Her attention was drawn to a small advertisement that was tucked away at the very bottom of the page. It began:

WAITRESSES – DOES LIFE SOMETIMES SEEM TO BE DULL AND PLAIN DOWNRIGHT BORING? AN EXCITING OPPORTUNITY HAS OCCURRED FOR A WAITRESS IN THE MOVIE INDUSTRY . . .

Kitty reached with one hand for the pencil which she always kept tucked into her hair and, with her other hand, she felt for the order-pad which swung, on a piece of string, from her waistbelt.

Carefully, she jotted down the telephone number at the end of the advertisement.

The Transylvanian Airways jet liner banked as it set its flight path for the final leg of the journey. The pilot had begun his descent and land was plainly visible below.

"Wow-eee*EEE*!" breathed Sharon Dexter, the blonde actress who had played the role of GIRL-IN-A-BIKINI in *Lobster Raiders*, as she gazed down out of the window next to her economy class seat in the jet liner. Then, turning to the man sitting beside her, she added: "Isn't this *exciting*, Harvey?"

"It sure is, Sharon," agreed Harvey Miskin, the shy bespectacled actor cast in the part of CHIEF LOBSTER, leaning over Sharon and daring to share with her the view out of the window.

The jet liner was passing over a vast Transylvanian snow-covered forest and flying low enough for them to be able to make out the tops of the snow-heavy pine trees. But it was not the scenery alone that had caused the pair's excitement. Recent events had brought about a thrilling upturn in the lives of

both Sharon Dexter and Harvey Miskin.

Sharon's role in *Lobster Raiders* had consisted of no more than a couple of scenes – one of which had been spent, mostly, crouching under a restaurant table – in *Dracula IS Dracula* she was to be given a much more substantial and important part. She had already been officially informed, by no less a person than the film's director, Howard Frost, that her role in the rewritten version would go from the beginning to the end of the movie – in the original film-script she had gone to her death in the claws of a vicious giant lobster raider as early as page seventeen.

As for Harvey Miskin, that actor could scarcely believe his own good fortune. For one thing, his part in the movie was being totally rewritten so that, instead of being the villain, the CHIEF LOBSTER was to become the hero. More than that though, Harvey told himself, he was sitting, at that moment, next to the most beautiful girl he had ever seen in his entire life. He had only one wish – it was that he might get to know her better.

Sitting in the rows behind and in front of Sharon and Harvey, were the other members of the film's company: actors; actresses; camera-crews; sound-men; make-up girls – all chattering excitedly as they drew closer to their destination.

From the rear of the economy class, Sharon and Harvey could hear the urgent tippety-tappety of a typewriter. The typewriter belonged to Chuck Cherwyn, the scriptwriter. Chuck was anxious to finish the new film-script before shooting began. His main task – apart from putting the vampire Count into the film – was to rewrite all the scenes originally intended to be shot on the sun-drenched Californian beaches into ones more suited to the Transylvanian snows.

"Can you keep a secret, Harvey?" asked Sharon Dexter, still gazing out of the window as the jet liner continued its descent.

"You can trust me, Sharon," replied the actor, his bright eyes blinking behind his glasses, delighted at being taken into the actress's confidence.

"Promise never to breath a word of this to a living soul," continued Sharon, dropping her voice. "But I'm really *scared* about doing this movie."

"How's that?"

"I've never acted in snow and ice before – I'm terrified that I'm gonna make a fool of myself and go slipping and sliding and losing my balance at all the important moments."

"Is that all?" replied Harvey, giving her a reassuring smile. "It'll be okay, Sharon, believe me, I'll look after you. I've done this kind of thing before.

126

I once played the part of an Eskimo."

"You did? *Wow!*" Sharon was impressed. Her eyes bulged. "Which film was that in?" she asked.

"It wasn't a film *exactly* – it was more in the nature of a TV commercial for *Mulligan's Ice-Cool Mints*. And it wasn't on real snow and ice either – we shot it on a studio-set with the floor covered in cotton wool." Harvey Miskin paused, blinked, summoned all of his courage, took hold of Sharon's hand and gave it a little reassuring squeeze before continuing, earnestly: "But it was real experience, Sharon, and if there is any way at all that I can help you while we're making *this* movie – well, you only have to ask."

"Thanks, Harvey."

"I really mean it, Sharon. Anything at all. If you want a cup of coffee or a hot dog bringing during a break, anything at all like that."

The actress turned from the window and smiled at the actor who was blinking furiously behind his glasses. Harvey Miskin gulped. He returned the smile as he noted, gratefully, that Sharon had made no attempt to detach her hand from his. Harvey Miskin gulped again and wondered whether something wonderful was about to happen in his life.

"We shall be arriving shortly at Botrograd Airport," the voice of the air hostess broke in on Harvey's daydreams, over the loudspeaker. "Would you kindly extinguish all cigarettes, return to your seats and fasten your seat-belts securely."

Hiram P. Hurtzburger sighed with relief as he made his way back to his seat in the first class cabin. He would soon have his feet on solid ground again.

127

The famous film producer hated flying. Not because he went in any fear of that activity – Hurtzburger's dislike of aircraft stemmed from the fact that cigar-smoking was forbidden in flight. Hurtzburger always spent his time when flying in pacing up and down the aisle, chewing nervously on an unlit cigar.

"Almost there, Hiram," said Hetty Hurtzburger as her husband eased his ample frame into the seat beside her. Mrs Hurtzburger always accompanied the film producer when he travelled abroad to make his movies – she liked to stay as close as possible to his cheque-book. "I can't make up my mind, honey," she continued. "I don't know whether to buy myself a fur coat in the airport giftshop as soon as we arrive – or wait until I can get to visit the stores where they're bound to have a better selection. Perhaps I'll do both and buy *two* fur coats."

"More fur coats," growled Hiram, grumpily. "You've got a wardrobe full of fur coats already."

"Not *Transylvanian* fur coats, Hiram. I don't have a single one of those – yet. What would you do if you were me?"

"I'd buy myself some woolly sweaters instead," growled the film producer, still chewing nervously on his unlit cigar, "and help conserve the wildlife."

The aircraft was now skimming low over the tips of the pine trees, on its final approach to Botrograd Airport. Hurtzburger shivered as he got his own first glimpse of the Transylvanian wildlife. A whole pack of lean and hungry wolves were loping through the forest below, plunging through the snowdrifts, their sharp fangs gleaming in the early afternoon sun.

"Won't be long now, Howie," said Hurtzburger,

128

shifting his glance from the window as he leaned forward and tapped the shoulder of the film director who was sitting in front of him. "I'll bet a million dollars you can't wait to start shooting in that wonderful scenery, huh?"

"There's only one thing worrying me, Mr Hurtzburger," said Howard Frost, glancing over the back of his seat. "I'm wondering whether we're going to have a star for the picture? Are you sure that this Count Alucard guy is going to turn up? Was it wise to let him make his own way over here?"

"Sure he's going to turn up, Howie. He gave me his solemn word. The word of a true Transylvanian count – and those kinda guys don't mess with words, Howie."

Hiram P. Hurtzburger had tried hard to hide his own concern. He too was worried as to whether Count Alucard would arrive in Transylvania for the first day's shooting. The famous film producer had tried to talk the Count into travelling on the aircraft with the rest of the film's company. He had even offered him a seat in the first class cabin with himself, his wife and the film's director. But the Count had turned down this attractive offer. He had insisted on making his own way from the United States back to his native land.

As it happened, the fears of the famous film producer and the director were entirely groundless. Not only would Count Alucard turn up in time for the first day of shooting – he had arrived some days before the rest of the company.

Count Alucard scrambled up onto the highest stone

that he could find and looked down the snow-covered mountainside towards the rooftops of the distant village. He was standing on the ruins of the once-proud Castle Alucard, his family home. The castle had been burned to the ground, long years before, by the angry villagers who had hated the very name "Alucard".

But the Count could not find it in his generous heart to blame the villagers for what they had done. He knew full well that his ancestors had been blood-drinking vampires. All the same, the Count reflected to himself and not for the first time, it was very sad that, all this time later, he was still having to suffer for the sins of his forebears. The Count blinked back a tear and blew his nose hard, as he considered the time that he had spent in exile from his native land. Then, shrugging away his sadness, he turned to thoughts of happier memories – for there were lots of those as well . . .

As a child, he had scampered through the warm-scented pine woods, paddled in the babbling mountain streams and raced helter-skelter down the mountainside. Because he had been shunned by the village children, he had befriended, instead, the creatures of the forest: the birds; the deer; the foxes and the rabbits – and, yes, he had even counted the wolves among his friends. Oh, yes indeed, there were many happy memories for the Count to dream upon . . .

It had been with this intention of revisiting old haunts and remembering past times, that the Count had insisted upon returning to Transylvania alone.

The journey back to Europe, from Los Angeles,

had taken far, far less time than his outward trip. This time he had not lingered at all *en route*. He had travelled by speeding goods train from California to New York, a three-day journey which he had spent, in his bat form, hanging upside-down underneath an empty truck, with the tips of his ears skimming inches over the railway sleepers. At New York's Kennedy Airport, he had managed to smuggle himself into the hold of an Italian jet liner bound for Rome. From Italy he had relied again on his own wing-power to carry him back to Transylvania.

Count Alucard had been back now in his native land for three whole days and, already, he was beginning to feel as if he really belonged . . .

"Good day to you, sir! May I beg a word of you?"

Count Alucard turned to find himself looking across at a small man with a big moustache who was shivering on the driving-seat of a horse-drawn waggon.

"It would be a poor sort of a world if a man were not to grant such a simple request to a passing stranger," replied the Count as he carefully eased himself down from the heap of snow-covered stones on which he had been standing.

"You wouldn't say that, friend, if you'd spent the last few hours with me." As he spoke, the man heaved a long, sad sigh which caused the little icicles dangling from his moustache to tremble.

"Why? What happened?"

"Before I begin to tell you, will you promise me one thing?" said the waggoner.

"If it is within my power."

"I want you to promise me not to turn and take

to your heels the moment that I ask you a simple question."

"And why on earth should I choose to do that?"

"Because that's exactly what everyone else has done that I have met this morning."

"Ah!" the Count spoke softly. "Then I think that I can hazard a guess as to the question that you have put to them?"

"If you can do that," said the man, "you must be some sort of mind-reader."

Count Alucard shook his head. "You don't come from around these parts, do you?"

It was the waggoner's turn to shake his head. "I've journeyed all the way from Botrograd," as he spoke, the man glanced over his shoulder and nodded at a large, oblong package on the back of his waggon. "I picked that up at Botrograd Railway Station early this morning. It's taken me the best part of two hours to drive over here. But you still haven't told me the nature of the question for which I am unable to get an answer?"

"You have been enquiring of the local folk the whereabouts of Alucard Castle."

"Great heavens preserve us!" cried the waggoner, shaking with surprise and causing the little icicles dangling from his moustache to tinkle together merrily. "You are a mind-reader!"

"Not at all," replied the Count with a smile. "But I understand the nature of people that live hereabouts. Also, I think I recognise the nature of that package on your waggon. I believe it is intended for myself. I am Count Alucard. This is Alucard Castle – or what is left of it. Come, friend, allow me to assist you to lower it to the ground – it is too heavy an object for one man alone to lift."

Some time later, after the man with the horse-and-waggon had gone on his way, the Count unfastened the stout rope and ripped away the cardboard covering which contained his coffin. Inside the polished black casket, pinned to the lace-edged, white satin pillow, he discovered a purple envelope addressed to himself in neat handwriting. Inside the envelope was a letter written on matching purple notepaper, which read:

Dear Count Alucard,

I hope that you will not think me a nosey-parkering old busybody. But as I had not heard from you for some time, I thought it might be best if I forwarded on your coffin. After all that upset with the villagers, they finally returned it to me. I don't imagine you will have been getting much of a good night's sleep without it. I think that I can safely report that the villagers are feeling ashamed of themselves now for having treated you so badly. And so they should! Speak as you find, I always say, and I always found you to be kindness itself. All that I would like to add is that if you should ever chance to pass this way again, you are more than welcome to your old room and bed-and-breakfast at Honeysuckle Cottage. Hoping this finds you as it leaves me.
Yours sincerely,

Thora Prendergast (Mrs)

The Count sat down on the coffin took out his

handkerchief and blew his nose, hard, for the second time that afternoon. Such acts of kindness were accorded him so infrequently that, when they did come his way, they touched him deeply. It was always heartening to discover, he told himself, that there was *some* goodness in the world. And, who could tell, perhaps when he had made the film that was to change his public image, there might be many people who would look upon him in the same light as the dear, dear old lady he was pleased to call his friend—

"Excuse me, mister?" piped up a small voice close at hand. "What's that big black thing you're sitting on?"

The Count had glanced up to find himself being confronted by two small children a boy and a girl, both wrapped up warmly against the wintry weather and staring inquisitively at his coffin.

"Is it a box for keeping things in?" asked the girl, the smaller of the two.

Count Alucard smiled and shook his head. So, there were children growing up now in the district who had not heard of the Dracula Legend? Children who were not afraid of walking up the mountainside and wandering close by the ruins of his ancestral home. And if those children were to grow up and have children of their own, similarly innocent and unafraid . . . Who knows? Perhaps, in years to come, the legend of the blood-drinking vampires might be lost altogether in the mists of time? The one thing that he must not do, the Count told himself, would be to frighten off this charming pair with talk of coffins.

"It is," he began, and paused – and thought – and then began again: "It is whatever I want it to be."

"Can it be a sledge?" asked the boy, eagerly.

"Oh, can it, *please*? *Please* let it be a sledge." The girl's voice rose, shrilly, with excitement.

"Why not?" replied the Count. "Hop aboard!"

Less than a minute later, with the two children sitting in front and the Count behind them, his gangly legs stretched out in front as he steered the smooth black casket with his feet, they had set off down the snow-covered mountain slopes, picking up speed as they went.

"Whhheee!" cried the children.

"WhhheeeEEE!" called out Count Alucard, the very last of the vampires, as the makeshift toboggan hurtled on, weaving in and out of the pine trees.

9

"This here's the darnedest fog I ever did come across," grumbled Sheriff Wayne Tucker to his deputy as he steered their hired car round yet another snow-covered left-hand bend. "Take another peek at that there road-map, Brad, and see iffen you can't make head nor tail of where we might be exactly."

"I surely will do that Sheriff," replied Bradford Crick, unfolding the tattered map which almost fell into pieces in his hands and which a crafty guard had been pleased to sell them at the Transylvanian border checkpoint. "But I can't quite figure out what good it's going to do us, Sheriff, finding out where we are, iffen we don't know where we're headed?"

Travelling unofficially and out of uniform, the two Kansas lawmen were pretending to be a couple of tourists. With this deception in mind, Wayne Tucker was dressed in Bermuda shorts and a shirt colourfully decorated with palm trees and blue lagoons; while Bradford Crick was wearing cut-down jeans and a teeshirt which had DISNEYLAND printed across its front together with a picture of Goofy. Their style of dress, they had long ago dis-

136

covered, was not suitable to the Transylvanian winter and they were hoping to pick up warmer clothing before they arrived at their destination – wherever that might be . . .

Their main problem was that they had no idea where they were going. The article, torn out of the movie magazine, which had given them the information that Count Alucard was to make a film in Transylvania, had not gone on to say in which particular *part* of Transylvania the filming was to take place. Transylvania, they had discovered, was a very big place. Not as big as Kansas, it was true, but more than big enough for them to lose themselves entirely. As neither of them could speak a word of Transylvanian – and as none of the Transylvanians they had so far encountered could speak a work of English – they were rather puzzled as to how they might track down their quarry. These difficulties being not at all assisted by the fact that they were driving along a snow-covered road, with many bends, and in thick fog.

"It surely wouldn't do any harm, Brad Crick, for us to find out where we are, at least," snapped the sheriff. "Then, if we should discover where we're going, we'd benefit by knowing where we were coming from. We're on some crazy kind of road that's all left bends." As he spoke, and as if to emphasise his words, Sheriff Tucker steered left again. "A road that seems to turn left every twenty yards or so, should sure as hell be easy to find on the map?"

"Not in this light, Sheriff," replied Crick with a shake of his head, holding up the open road-map towards the car window and squinting at it with one eye shut.

To add to their miseries, it had begun to snow again. The big snowflakes hugged the windscreen, causing the windscreen wiper to squeal and stutter in its attempts to shift them.

"This here's no good at all, Brad," sighed Sheriff Tucker. "I'm gonna pull over by the roadside and you can see iffen you climb up that there stone wall and see what you can see?"

They had been driving by the side of the same stone wall, it seemed, for quite some time. Because of the fog, they were unable to see the top of the wall and had no idea of what was on its other side.

"Are you asking me to climb a wall, Sheriff?" shivered Bradford Crick as he gazed forlornly at the falling snow out of the parked car's window. "In this kinda weather and in a teeshirt?"

"I don't know who else I'm asking, Brad Crick, iffen it ain't you!" said the sheriff, rather sharply. "I certainly ain't figuring on climbing up that wall myself. That ain't no job for a sheriff – leastways, not when he's got a deputy to do the climbing for him. Now, just you do as I've told you, Bradford Crick!"

"I thought this was to be some kind of vacation," grumbled Crick to himself, but not quite loud enough for the sheriff to hear. Then, getting out of the car, he crossed to the base of the stone wall and, still shivering, began to climb up, slowly, handhold after icy handhold. Luckily, he did not have very far to climb. The wall, he discovered, was only about three metres high and, once on top, he found himself in for several surprises.

"Well, I'll be hog-tied!" he murmured to himself, and then he called out, loudly, to the car which was hidden in the fog below: "Hey, Sheriff! This ain't no wall at all! This here's the base of a statue and we must have been driving round and round it – that's why we've been making so many left-hand turns. We've been going round and round in circles, Sheriff!"

"What kind of a statue is it, Brad?" The sheriff's voice came from out of the gloom below.

"Well, first of all, there's an old guy with a beard and he's holding up an umbrella and he's standing by a chair and then sitting down on the chair there's a—"

"I'll thank you to mind your manners, Bradford Crick, and not start calling *me* a statue!" said the lady sitting on the chair.

139

"Well, I'll be *double* hog-tied!" gasped the Deputy Sheriff.

"What is it, Brad?" the voice of Sheriff Tucker drifted up again from the ground below.

"You ain't a-gonna believe this, Sheriff!" the deputy called down. "The old guy with the beard and the umbrella, he's a statue sure enough – but the lady sitting on the chair, she *ain't* no statue . . . Prepare yourself for a shock, Sheriff, when I tell you who I've found up here – it's Kitty!"

"Kitty who?" the sheriff called back.

"Kitty from Kansas!" called down the waitress from the roadside diner. "Kitty Beaumont! Kitty who-else? Just how many Kittys do you know, Sheriff Tucker?"

"Well, I'll be *double* hog-tied too!" murmured Wayne Tucker.

"It sure comes as some surprise, Kitty, bumping into you on top of a statue in Transylvania," said Bradford Crick. "I thought you was back home in Kansas."

"I was just about to say the very same thing to you, Brad Crick," replied the pretty waitress. "What are you doing here anyways?"

"I climbed up to find out where we were exactly," explained the deputy sheriff. "We got lost in all this fog. What are *you* doing up here?"

"I was waiting for a bus—" began Kitty.

"On top of a *statue*?" broke in Crick.

"No! I was waiting for a bus when it began to snow. I climbed up here to shelter." The waitress nodded at the statue's umbrella, then at the chair. "And to rest my tired feet," she added. "It seems

140

like I've been walking for miles."

"Whereabouts are you headed for Kitty?"

"I'm going to a little village called Rumptoft.
I don't suppose that you're going anywhere near
there?"

"To tell the truth, Kitty," admitted the sheriff's
deputy, "we're not entirely certain, right at this
moment, exactly where we *are* going."

"Are you two planning on spending all day up
there?" the sheriff called up from the car. "The
snow's stopped and the fog's beginning to lift. It's
high time we were on our way, Brad."

"I'll be right there, Sheriff!" the deputy called
back. "Do you suppose we might give Kitty here a
lift? She's headed for a place called Rumptoft."

"Can't see why not," the sheriff replied. "I guess
that one place is just as good as any other, as far as
we're concerned."

Bradford Crick flashed Kitty a grin, picked up
her suitcase which she had previously put down
beside the statue's chair, and then offered her his
hand to help her scramble down from the statue's
base.

"I hope you won't think I'm being inquisitive,
Kitty," said Sheriff Tucker, over his shoulder,
several minutes later when they were all three in the
car and headed along the country road. "But just
what brings you to Transylvania? And why exactly
are you going to this one-horse Rumptoft joint?"

"Why, no, Sheriff, I don't mind telling you at
all." As she spoke, the waitress fished inside her
handbag and took out the page from the movie
magazine containing the advertisement which had

141

caught her eye. "Scary Films Incorporated are making a movie there. They needed a waitress to serve the meals to all the actors and the actresses. Guess what? I got the job!"

"That's swell, Kitty!" said Bradford Crick. "I guess that's gonna be a whole heap more exciting than dishing up coffee and doughnuts to the sheriff and me in that there Kansas diner. What do you say, Sheriff?"

But Sheriff Tucker did not reply. He was busy putting two and two together.

"Did you say that they were making that there movie in this here Rumptoft?"

"Uh-huh. I surely did, Sheriff. Will you two be staying in Rumptoft for a while?"

"Nope." Sheriff Tucker shook his head, firmly. "I only wish we could, Kitty. But Brad and me have got a whole lot of sightseeing to do. As soon as we've dropped you off, we'll be on our way." But as he spoke, and unseen by Kitty, Sheriff Tucker turned and gave his deputy a sly wink, indicating that he was telling the waitress less than the truth.

It had stopped snowing completely. As the sheriff put his foot down on the accelerator, the two inches of white covering that lay on the road crunched comfortably underneath the wheels.

The snow had stopped falling too on the mountain-side above the village of Rumptoft. Count Alucard waved goodbye to Konrad and Gretel, the two children who had befriended him and with whom he had pleasantly passed the entire afternoon, sledging on the upper slopes on his improvised toboggan.

The Count was pleased with life. In the course of one afternoon he had not only had his precious coffin returned to him, he had also made two new friends. What was even more important, he was back in the district where he had been born and raised. He was home. What the villagers would say when they discovered that an Alucard was back amongst them was an altogether different matter. But that could wait. He trusted that his good friend, Mr Hurtzburger, would keep that piece of information from the villagers, at least for the time being.

Pushing the coffin before him across the smooth snow, the Count set off towards the ruins of the Castle Alucard. He had noticed earlier that, by pushing aside a couple of large stones, he would have access to the castle's dungeons. He could sleep down there for the time being. The Transylvanian nights were cold at this time of the year, but he would sleep warm inside his satin-padded casket.

Count Alucard turned and looked down the gentle slopes and gave a last wave at the two children who were now well on their way back home. Beyond the children, in the village square below, the Count could just make out what looked to him like a party of ants emerging from two matchboxes. These were, he rightly guessed, the members of the film company arriving from the airport in their charter-buses. The next day would see the start of his new career as a film star.

Returning to his task of pushing his coffin over the upper slopes towards the ruined castle, Count Alucard began to whistle, cheerfully.

"Hey, Hetty! You wanna know something? This is great stuff!" enthused Hiram P. Hurtzburger as he eagerly scanned the pages of the new script which Chuck Cherwyn had given him.

"I'm pleased to hear that, honey," murmured Hetty Hurtzburger, admiring herself in the big wardrobe mirror of the largest bedroom in Rumptoft's only inn. Mrs Hurtzburger had not only bought herself the most expensive fur coat on offer at the Transylvanian airport's gift shop, she had also purchased a new fur hat to match.

"You want I should read you some of the new scenes?" asked the famous film producer who was sitting up in bed, dressed in a pair of Paisley-patterned silk pyjamas, puffing on a cigar and reading by the warm glow of a bedside oil-lamp.

"Not just now, honey," replied Mrs Hurtzburger as she reluctantly took off the hat and coat in order to prepare for bed.

It was only nine o'clock but already the lamps were being turned down all over the village. There was not a great deal to do in Rumptoft, to pass the time, once the sun had slipped down behind the mountain. Coupled with which, there was to be an early start to the first day of shooting on the film the next morning. The actors, actresses, camera crews and all the rest, who had been found lodgings not only at the inn but in guest-houses all over the village, were happy to follow the example set by the villagers and settle for an early night.

"Aw, c'mon, Hetty – let me just read you one scene before we go to sleep," implored Hiram P. Hurtzburger. "How about the one where the vampire sneaks into the orphanage and kills three kids before the lobster leader arrives and beats the living daylights outta the brute?"

"Oh, very well, Hiram," agreed Hetty Hurtzburger as she slipped between the bed's rough sheets. Mrs Hurtzburger was not that interested in her husband's films – apart from recognising their potential in providing her with new fur coats.

"*Scene 32 – The Orphanage – Night,*" began the film producer, reading from the script. "*The full moon is hidden behind a black cloud as we see the vampire creep across the orphanage's well-trimmed lawn, snarling and growling and flashing its pointy fangs* . . .

On the top floor of the village inn, in a room far smaller than the one occupied by the Hurtzburgers, in a single brass bed, Sharon Dexter was fast asleep and dreaming about being a movie star while, in the room next to her's, Harvey Miskin was dreaming about Sharon Dexter. ➡

Across the village square, in the tiny guest-bedroom of a small lodging-house, Kitty Beaumont, the pretty waitress, lay fast asleep and dreaming – a strange dream in which she was standing on the base of a statue, tossing doughnuts by the bucketful to a horde of hungry actors and actresses who were clamouring on a rock below, clapping their hands and barking like hungry seals.

On the lower slopes of the snow-covered mountain, in a small tent which they had pitched under a fringe of pine trees, Sheriff Wayne Tucker and Deputy Sheriff Bradford Crick lay side by side in their sleeping-bags, tossing fitfully and too uncomfortable to sleep deeply enough to dream.

Higher up the mountain, in an arched stone dungeon underneath the ruins of the Castle Alucard, the vegetarian vampire Count lay snug and warm in his coffin and gazed up through a gap in the stonework at the star-filled sky. Count Alucard was far too excited to sleep at all. He was looking forward impatiently to starting work on the film. From far away, he could hear the wolf-pack baying at the moon. But such sounds didn't worry the Count – having grown up with the wolves he counted each and every one of them his friend. Their howling was like music to his ears.

"That took some time!" grumbled Alphonse Kropotel, the village police sergeant at his wife as she tiptoed down the worn wooden bedroom staircase. As Kropotel spoke, the small wooden bird whirred out of the carved cuckoo clock on the wall above the smoking pot-bellied stove and "Cuck-ooed" once to say that it was half-past nine.

"You don't need to tell me how long it's taken," replied Irma Kropotel with a sigh. "You just wouldn't believe the trouble I've had in getting those two children to settle down tonight."

"I can't think why," Kropotel paused, spat into the tin of black boot polish, rubbed some of the polish onto an already shiny boot, before continuing: "You'd have thought that they'd have been

146

tired out – the amount of time they spent playing up there on the mountain this afternoon."

"It's because of the mountain that I couldn't get them to settle," explained the plump Mrs Kropotel. "They had such an enjoyable time up there, they wouldn't stop chattering about it."

"Why? What happened?" the police sergeant polished briskly at his boot with a stiff brush.

"Oh, something and nothing," replied his wife with a shrug which caused her heavy shoulders to wobble. "They were chattering on about some man they met up there by the castle ruins – but, if you want my opinion, I think he exists only in their imaginations."

"The ruins of the Castle Alucard?" Alphonse Kropotel rubbed harder and angrily. "How many times have I told those two that they mustn't go anywhere near those ruins?"

"You're living in the past, Alphonse," replied Mrs Kropotel with another shrug, and this time all her several chins wobbled. "The Alucards are dead and gone."

"Gone, yes – dead, maybe," said Kropotel, putting one boot down and starting work on the other. "We cannot be certain. It doesn't do to take chances. Who was this man they met up there?"

"I've already told you, Alphonse. I don't believe that there was a man. I think they made him up."

"What makes you say that?"

"Because of the way that they described him," said Irma Kropotel, and this time her shoulders and her chins both wobbled at the same time as she chuckled, then went on: "What kind of a man would

147

go out on a snowy mountain wearing a black suit, a starched white shirt, a black bow tie and a black cloak with a crimson lining? I ask you!"

"What kind of a man!" thundered the police sergeant, leaping so high to his feet that he almost bumped his head on the low-beamed ceiling. "I'll tell you what kind of a man, Irma – a vampire, that's who! The man that you have just described to me is an Alucard without a shadow of a doubt!" Kropotel paused to cross himself, fearfully. "God preserve us, wife – there is one of them back amongst us!"

"But he can't be, Alphonse," replied Mrs Kropotel, every ounce of her spare flesh a-tremble. "The children said that this man was kindness itself towards them. Why, he took them sledging on a long black box which had silver handles and . . ." her voice trailed away as she realised the implications, then: "Oh, my heavens!" and "All the Saints preserve us!" she murmured.

"And praise those same Saints too, wife, for letting us know about him in time," snapped Kropotel as he pulled on his boots. "Why, if those children had ventured up onto those slopes tomorrow, be sure he would have had his pointy teeth into their poor little necks!"

"You're surely not going out tonight, Alphonse?" asked Irma Kropotel as her husband got to his feet and reached for his belt from which hung the holster containing his police revolver.

"I must. Something has to be done about that evil monster."

"But you're not going to . . ." Mrs Kropotel

paused, and this time her entire ample body wobbled as her eyes glanced nervously through the window and towards the mountain.

"Of course not, wife! What do you take me for? I'm not going anywhere near those ruins tonight. I'm stepping round to tell Henri Rumboll what we've learned."

"You're going to see the mayor?" asked Irma Kropotel. "At this hour? He'll be sound asleep."

"Then I shall wake him up," said Sergeant Kropotel, firmly. "He'll decide what needs to be done – and tomorrow morning we shall take that action as soon as it is light." Police Sergeant Kropotel crossed to the door, slid open the bolt and then paused before lifting the latch. "And a word of warning to you, Irma – no one else must know about this."

"Who could I tell, if I wanted to?" asked Mrs Kropotel, scornfully. "I shan't be seeing anyone."

"I know what you are, when it comes to gossip," growled her husband. "And we can't be too careful – particularly with all these strangers in the village. If they should get to hear that there is a real, live, blood-drinking vampire hereabouts, they'll be on their way. Taking their wallets with them. These are the first visitors we've seen in these parts in years. So just remember – it's a secret."

With which, after gulping twice, Police Sergeant Alphonse Kropotel strode out into the Transylvanian night, trying hard to look brave.

Left alone in her tiny living-room, Irma Kropotel crossed quickly to the door and shot the wooden bolt back into place. Then, moving to the window, she peered up towards the top of the snow-covered mountain which was glittering in the light of the moon. Far off in the distance, she thought that she could hear the baying of the wolf-pack.

Shivering, the police sergeant's wife drew the curtains and then pulled a rough-made wooden stool close up to the pot-bellied stove. Mrs Kropotel rarely chose to sit near the stove. The smoke which belched out through the many cracks caused her to cough. But tonight she sat as close to the stove as possible. She put out her hands towards the glowing logs and tried to draw some comfort from the warmth.

10

"Are you sure that the evil creature is back in our midst?" whispered Henri Rumboll, the mayor of Rumptoft, to Alphonse Kropotel as the two men laboured up the side of the mountain.

"As sure as God is my maker," muttered the police sergeant, crossing himself as he spoke as protection against the vampire.

The two men had waited, before starting out, until the first rays of the early morning sun were casting their golden glow across the snow-covered slopes. But they were neither of them in a mood to appreciate the wintry scenic beauty as they struggled to put one foot in front of the other, encountering snowdrift after snowdrift. In order not to give their approach away to the vampire, they had chosen to ignore the regular footpath and to make their way, instead, up the untrodden slopes. It was proving to have been a foolhardy decision.

"Listen!" hissed Kropotel, after they had stumbled on in silence for some time. "Did you hear something?"

Receiving no reply, the police sergeant glanced towards his companion – but was shocked to discover that the mayor had disappeared completely.

Kropotel was horrified. Was it possible, he wondered, for a vampire to snatch his victim away into thin air? Shivering both with cold and fear the police sergeant gazed all around, open-mouthed.

"Don't just stand there staring, you fool! Help me up!"

The mayor's voice seemed to come from out of the ground and the police sergeant glanced down to discover that Rumboll had sunk into a snowdrift.

"I thought I heard something up ahead," hissed Kropotel after he had assisted the mayor up onto his feet again.

Moving forward, slowly, through snow and pine trees, the two men crested a rise to find, to their surprise, that although they had set out at the crack of dawn, others had been up and about before them.

Peering through a clump of bushes hung with lacy frost, Kropotel and Rumboll watched as a group of men began to set up arc-lamps and cameras in a clearing on the wooded slopes, in readiness for the start of the first day of filming. Other workmen were putting up huts and tents for use as dressing-areas, make-up tents and temporary offices.

"Why didn't you tell me they were coming up here this morning?" whispered Rumboll, testily.

"How was I to know?" replied Kropotel. "They didn't inform me of their intentions. What does it matter to us anyway? We can walk straight past them."

"And where shall we tell them we are going, at this time of morning, if they ask?"

"Looking for mushrooms?"

"In the middle of winter?" hissed the mayor. "If they get so much as a sniff of what we're doing here, they'll be on their way."

"Speaking of sniffing," whispered Kropotel, hungrily licking his lips. "Can you smell bacon frying?"

Mayor Rumboll nodded, his own mouth watering, and pointed across at where a group of actors and actresses were gathered around the unit's catering van, stamping their feet on the hard-packed snow, munching bacon-rolls and drinking hot coffee. Neither the mayor nor the police sergeant had eaten before setting out that morning and the delicious smell of frying bacon on the crisp air was almost too much for both of them. As if to torture himself even more, Alphonse Kropotel took the pair of binoculars from out of the leather case which was hung around his neck and focussed them on the rashers of bacon which were sizzling in the big frying-pan behind the counter of the catering-van.

Strange to tell, but Alphonse Kropotel was not the only police officer to have binoculars trained on that very same frying-pan full of bacon. On another side of the clearing, hidden behind another clump of bushes, Sheriff Wayne Tucker had got his own binoculars firmly focussed on the appetizing sight.

"Gosh darn it, Sheriff! Let me take a peek," pleaded Crick, holding out his hand for the binoculars. "I'm starving."

The two Kansas lawmen had been disturbed from their uncomfortable night's sleep by the sounds of the film unit arriving up the mountain path. They had barely had time to struggle out of their sleeping bags, hastily put on the rough peasant clothing they had bought the previous afternoon, and strike their tent, before the clearing had begun to fill with movie people. Like Alphonse Kropotel and Henri Rumboll, Wayne Tucker and Bradford Crick had not had any food pass their lips that morning.

"That there Kitty," murmured Sheriff Tucker, peering through the binoculars at the waitress who was hard at work behind the catering-van's counter. "She surely does know how to rustle up a bacon-roll!"

"She surely does, Sheriff!" murmured his deputy, wistfully, wishing himself back home and sitting up at the counter of the roadside diner, ordering breakfast.

Over at the van, Kitty Beaumont, unaware of the four pairs of hungry eyes that were watching her, laid several rashers of bacon alongside several others which were sizzling and spitting, merrily, in the frying-pan.

"Could I have a bacon-roll, please? And a coffee?"

"Coming right up!" said Kitty, turning and smiling down at Sharon Dexter who had already been both to costume and to make-up and was ready and waiting to begin work.

"Coffee and bacon-rolls for two," said a messenger-boy, importantly, as he squeezed his way up to the head of the queue and stood on tiptoe in order to peer over the counter. "They're for Mr Hurtzburger and Mr Frost, so make 'em snappy – and they want the bacon crispy and the coffee hot!"

"Sorry, honey," said Kitty, with an apologetic smile at Sharon. "But this is my first day on the job – so I guess the boss comes first."

"I guess he does," replied Sharon, wrinkling her nose in disappointment.

Over in the largest tent, which was being used as the production office, Hiram P. Hurtzburger and Howard Frost waited impatiently for the arrival of their breakfasts – and more impatiently for the arrival of the star of the film.

"It's gone seven o'clock, Mr Hurtzburger," said the film director, glancing at his watch, "and there's still no sign of this guy Alucard."

"He'll *be* here, Howie," replied the famous film producer, none too surely. "He gave me his word and, like he told me and I told you, the word of an Alu—"

"What do you think, Hiram!" broke in the voice of Mrs Hurtzburger, who was standing in a corner

155

of the tent, admiring herself in her new fur coat and her new fur hat. "Does it suit me better *with* the belt – or should I take it off?"

"Not right now, Hetty," groaned Hurtzburger, biting through the end of his cigar in his impatience. "Give me a break, huh? I'm trying to get a movie off the ground."

Hetty Hurtzburger, knowing full well that getting movies off the ground were preliminaries to getting fur coats onto her back, wisely held her tongue.

But the joint concern of Hurtzburger and his director with regard to the non-arrival of the star of their film was totally unnecessary. Count Alucard was on his way.

"Holy molony, Sheriff!" murmured Bradford Crick, peering through the binoculars at the dark shape which was speeding down the mountainside. "Will you just take a look at that!"

"That's him, Brad," snapped Sheriff Tucker, having taken the binoculars and focussed them on the black object which was hurtling down the snow-covered slopes, weaving in and out of the pine trees and drawing closer with every second.

Count Alucard, having spent most of the previous night wide-awake and relaxing in the comfort of his coffin, gazing up at the night-sky and listening to his friends, the wolves, had finally fallen asleep in the early hours of the morning and had then over-slept. For that reason, in order not to be late for his first day at his new job, he had chosen to toboggan down the mountainside to join the film unit. In order to travel even faster than before, he had streamlined his makeshift sledge of the day before and was tobogganing only on the coffin's lid.

Lying stomach-down, head-first and full-length on the coffin-top, the Count was zapping down the slopes and steering with his shiny black-patent-leather-shod feet which were stretched out behind him. With both his wide black cloak and his usually neat long black hair blowing in the wind, the Count presented an awesome sight as he bounded onwards on the coffin-lid. Sometimes he would take off into the air as he shot over the edge of a small snow-ledge and then bounce down again, hitting the soft snow up ahead, picking up speed as he went.

"Mercifulheaven!" murmured Alphonse Kropotel, the police sergeant, who had also picked up the Count's approach through his binoculars. "Perhaps now you will admit that I was right," he added, passing the binoculars to Henri Rumboll.

"God preserve us!" muttered the mayor, giving a little shudder. "You were right, Alphonse – the vampire *has* come back to Rumptoft to torment us."

Both men shifted uncomfortably in their cramped hiding-place in the clump of bushes as they heard, carried on the wind but from not *too* far away, the howling of the wolf-pack in the forest.

"Listen to that!" said Kropotel. "They know that he has come back too. What are we to do, Mayor Rumboll? Should we . . ." he paused and swallowed hard, then began again: ". . . Should we arrest him the moment that he comes to a stop?"

"No," Henri Rumboll slowly shook his head. He was not anxious for a confrontation with the vampire himself. "We will bide our time, Sergeant. The element of surprise is ours. The evil creature does

157

not know that we are onto him. We shall wait – and make our move when the time is right."

Not far away, in another clump of bushes, the two Kansas lawmen were arriving at a similar decision themselves. Sheriff Tucker and Deputy Crick were totally unaware that Mayor Rumboll and Sergeant Kropotel were also in hiding, quite close to where they were themselves and in a similar clump of bushes. But then, Rumboll and Kropotel were equally unaware of the presence of Tucker and Crick.

"What's the plan, Sheriff?" asked Crick, rather nervously, as he watched the Count speed closer on his coffin-top sledge. "Do we move in right away and arrest the vampire as soon as he gets here?"

"No way, Brad," replied the sheriff with a long, slow shake of his head. Now that he was about to come face to face with the Count again, Sheriff Tucker was beginning to feel a little nervous himself. He shivered slightly as he recalled the manner in which the creature had disappeared, mysteriously and in the twinkling of an eye, from out of the county-jail's locked cell. "Ain't no sense in rushing into anything – let's you an' me just bide our time and make our move exactly when it suits—" Sheriff Tucker broke off as the howling of the wolf-pack rose up again on the crisp morning air. "There it goes again, Brad!"

"It surely does, Sheriff," gulped the deputy, shuffling his behind uneasily on the prickly bed of pine needles. "And if you ask me, those danged critturs sound closer than they did the last time!"

Count Alucard, who had no idea that two separate sets of officials were waiting to apprehend him, felt his spirits soar as he sped out from a fringe of pine trees and the blazing arc-lights of the film unit came into sight. He was, he told himself, about to embark on the most important and exciting day of the whole of his life . . .

"You can't expect me to agree to this!" said the Count, horrified. He was sitting in the production tent, his thin shoulders slumped, his pale slim hands trembling as he clutched the pages of the script he had been reading. "This is nothing like the story I was given to understand that we would film."

"That's show business, Dracky," chuckled Hiram P. Hurtzburger, rubbing the billiard-ball smoothness on the top of his head. "We've had to make some changes to the script since last we met."

"But you've got me biting people on the neck and drinking their blood . . ." Count Alucard gave a little shiver of distaste. "It just isn't my nature to behave like that."

"Aw, c'mon!" the famous film producer puffed on his cigar. "It's only a movie."

"But you said that it was going to show me as I really am," continued the Count. "And what about this scene where I break into an orphanage at night and kill little children?"

"Not *all* of the kids inside there, Drack-baby. You only get to polish off three kids – two girls one boy, in their pyjamas – and then the eight-foot Lobster Leader turns up and gives you one heck of a pasting."

"There are no eight-foot lobsters in Transylvania," replied the Count, icily. "Nor anywhere else

159

to the best of my knowledge."

"It's a horror movie, Drac," replied the famous film producer, extending his hands palm-upwards, wide. "It ain't supposed to be *history*."

"I'm sorry, Mr Hurtzburger," said Count Alucard, rising to his feet and putting the script down on the famous film producer's table. "I do apologise for any inconvenience I may have caused you – but I feel it only right and proper to tell you, here and now, that I sadly fear I cannot associate myself with your movie-making venture. However, I feel sure that you will easily obtain the services of an experienced professional actor who will be able to portray the character as you see it—"

"Forget it, Alucard!" Hurtzburger's smile had vanished. His brow was furrowed from his heavy eyebrows up past the start of his shiny bald head. The end of his cigar glowed fiercely red as his jaws conveyed it angrily from one side of his mouth to the other, then back again. "I signed you up to make this picture – and there's no way that you're gonna wriggle out of it."

"Not so, Mr Hurtzburger!" replied the Count, defiantly. "The film in which I agreed to appear was one that was going to show me as the sort of person that I really am. You gave me your solemn promise—"

"Promises are one thing, Dracky-baby," smirked the famous film producer, "but contracts are a different matter entirely!" As he spoke, Hurtzburger reached inside his overcoat pocket and produced the several pages of the official document to which the Count had put his signature, back in Los Angeles, some weeks before. "Didn't you take the trouble to read the small print!"

"I didn't even take the trouble to read the big print," replied the Count, uneasily. "I trusted you."

" '*The party of the first part,*' that's you," began Hurtzburger, peering through a magnifying glass at the last page of the contract, " '*hereby solemnly agrees to do everything required of him by the party of the second part*' that's me, '*etcetera, etcetera . . .*' I won't bore you with the finer details – but I've had the studio lawyers check this over and you can take my word for it, Drack old buddy, it's watertight. You're working for Hiram P. Hurtzburger now – and you'll do exactly as you're told."

"And supposing I refuse," said the Count, stiffly. "You can't *make* me act in your movie."

"Refuse?" chuckled Hurtzburger, throwing his hands up in the air in mock horror. "*You?* Break your contract? Break your *word?* The word of an Alucard? Your word, Drack old buddy, as you have said yourself, is something you would never go back on. And if you did break that contract, Dracky, I would see to it personally that the boys in my publicity department would give you such a bad name that you would never show your face in public again."

"You wouldn't do that, surely?" said Count Alucard, shocked at the proposal.

"Nope," replied the famous film producer with the hint of a smile. "Of course I wouldn't – just so long as you stick to what's written in that contract. But walk away from this picture, Dracky-baby, and you're in serious trouble. Break that contract and

161

my publicity boys will break you. If you think you don't have many friends today, because of who you are, believe me, when my press office has been to work on you, there won't be a single solitary man, woman or child across the face of this earth that would want to be in the same room as you. Think about it, Alucard. But don't do your thinking in my office – I'm busy. And don't take too long in making your mind up either. We start shooting the first scene in five minutes from now. Better get yourself across to make-up. Tell 'em I said to make those eyes of yours look a little bit spookier – and get 'em to put some fake blood on your chin, so's it looks as if you've just made an appetizing meal out of a couple of orphan kids, huh?"

It was a downcast Count Alucard that came out of Hurtzburger's tent. He was so downcast, in fact, that he failed to notice that Kitty, the waitress, was waving across at him from behind the counter of her catering-van.

"If that don't beat everything!" murmured Kitty, as she handed a bacon-roll to Sharon across the counter of the catering-van.

"What's that?" mumbled the actress biting eagerly into her appetising hot snack.

"Why, seeing him again," said the waitress, nodding across at where the Count was sitting deep in thought on the stump of a tree. "Would you believe it? I've travelled halfway around the world and that's the second time in less than twenty-four hours that I've met somebody I knew back home in Kansas. Wouldn't you say that that was some kind of wild coincidence?"

But Sharon made no reply. Her attention was elsewhere. She was looking across at Harvey Miskin who had just come out of the make-up tent. Harvey, in his lobster costume and with his feet encased in huge plastic lobster claws, was having difficulty in keeping his balance as he tried to walk across the hardpacked snow. It was much more difficult, he was discovering, to cross real snow and ice dressed as a lobster, than it had been to cross a studio floor covered with cotton wool in Eskimo costume. Sharon strove to hide a smile as she saw Harvey's eyes blinking uncertainly behind his glasses and inside his lobster head as, with both lobster-claw arms outstretched, he attempted to stay upright.

"Just take a look at him!" chuckled Sharon, as Harvey made unsteady progress towards the catering-van.

But it was Kitty's turn to hold her silence. The waitress was deep in thought. Putting two and two together, she realised that it was probably no coincidence that Wayne Tucker and Bradford Crick were both in Transylvania at the same time as Count Alucard. It was not difficult for the waitress to work out the real reason why the two Kansas lawmen were in Transylvania.

"I'll wager a small slice of Lemon Meringue Pie to a whole Cranberry Upside-Down Cake that Sheriff Tucker and Deputy Crick ain't holidaying here at all – they've come all this way to arrest that poor, polite Count Alucard . . ." murmured Kitty Beaumont to herself. Then, remembering that it was she herself that was responsible for bringing the two Kansas law officers to the film unit in Rumptoft, she

163

allowed her eyes to flit around the nearby wooded slopes and bushes, to see if Tucker and Crick were laying in wait. "Why – I'll also wager one Cranberry Upside-Down Cake to a whole barrelful of oatmeal cookies that that's them over there!" she added as she spotted two heads peering over the top of a clump of not-far-distant bushes.

In fact, although she was not far wrong – for the two Kansas lawmen were in hiding near where she stood – the waitress was also not quite right. The two heads that she had spotted emerging over the nearby undergrowth belonged, as it happened, to Police Sergeant Kropotel and Mayor Rumboll.

Alphonse Kropotel and Henri Rumboll had chosen to raise their heads, at the very moment that Kitty had glanced in that direction, in order to peer back down the slopes towards the village which nestled at the foot of the mountain. Something had attracted their attention. Peering back, down the snowy slopes, they could now make out what looked to be the entire male population of the village trudging upwards. What was more intriguing, the villagers seemed to be carrying makeshift weapons. Some of them were brandishing pitchforks; others were holding scythes; several, it appeared, were waving rakes or garden hoes above their heads.

"Mother of God!" gasped Alphonse Kropotel, blinking in astonishment. "What's happened?"

"A curse upon you and your family, Kropotel!" replied Henry Rumboll, angrily. "I'll tell you what's happened, Sergeant. It's that wife of yours again. She can't control her tongue. She's let the cat out of the bag and told everyone that the vampire is back amongst us!"

"No, no!" murmured the police sergeant. "She can't have done. She wouldn't."

"And I tell you that she not only would – she *has*!" snapped the mayor. "Why else do you imagine that the entire village is heading this way?"

It was true. Irma Kropotel had waited only until her husband and his companion had set off out of the square and up the road that led to the mountain, before she herself had gone out into the street knocking first on one door, then the next, informing her neighbours of the awful news. An Alucard had returned to torment them. Their children were not safe any longer. The lives of their old folk were in imminent danger.

Already, the angry cries of the villagers were beginning to carry up the mountainside on the morning breeze.

"Death to the monster!" "Down with the vampire!" "Destroy the evil creature!" "Kill him!" "Kill him!"

"How many times have I told you never to tell that woman anything?" snarled Mayor Rumboll as he watched the band of villagers moving slowly up the mountain path.

But Alphonse Kropotel was not listening. "Look!" murmured the police sergeant, tugging at the mayor's sleeve, happy to change the subject. "What do you make of that?"

Mayor Rumboll shifted his gaze from the approaching visitors and followed the police sergeant's glance. He was forced to admit that he did not know *what* to make of what he saw. Not far away, in a hiding-place similar to the one in which he and Kropotel were concealed, Henri Rumboll could see a pair of heads peering over the top of some bushes – in just the same way, in fact, that he and the police sergeant were peering over their own clump of bushes, except that while Kropotel and himself had been gazing *down* the mountain, these other two men seemed to be looking at something higher up the slopes.

"Who are they?" whispered Kropotel. "What are they doing here?"

Mayor Rumboll shook his head. He had no idea of the identity of the two strangers, nor had he the slightest notion as to the reason for their being there.

Sheriff Tucker and Deputy Crick, meanwhile, had no idea that they had been spotted. Their attention was firmly fixed on something in the pine trees which was causing them some concern.

"What do you think, Sheriff?" asked Bradford Crick anxiously. "Are they going to attack us?"

"Search me, Brad," muttered the sheriff, trying hard not to sound as frightened as he felt. "I don't know what they're gonna do – I've never been this close to a pack of wolves before – except when they've been penned in, safe and sound, on the right side of a zoo enclosure."

As far as the wolves themselves were concerned, it was the first time in many a long year that they had ventured so far down the mountain. The need had not arisen. For as long as they could remember, the wolves had shown as much respect for the villagers as the villagers had shown towards them. There had never been any cause for the animals to

166

antagonise the humans – and *vice versa*. Even in the harshest winter, there had always been sufficient game in the forest and fish in the streams for the wolf-pack to survive – without the need to venture down the slopes and steal from man. The villagers, in their turn, so long as their ducks and geese and hens were left unmolested, had seen no reason to venture anywhere near the wolves.

What it was, exactly that had lured the wolf-pack down from the thickly forested upper slopes on that particular morning would be difficult to say. Perhaps, initially, during the previous moonlit night, they had sensed the presence in the area of their old friend and ally, Count Alucard. Then, having sniffed and padded their way as far as the ruined castle in the morning's early light, their curiosity might have been stirred by their glimpsing the occasional flashes from the film unit's arc-lamps through the trees. Then, venturing even further down the mountainside, they could have been further intrigued by the sight of the ample figure of Hetty Hurtzburger as she strolled along the fringe of the forest. It is possible that they might have mistaken her, from a distance in her new fur coat and fur hat, for some strange animal that had trespassed into their territory – for while they were willing to live alongside human beings without quarrelling, the wolves were ever quick to attack any animals that sought to invade their domain. Then, having got that far, they could have been tempted further by the delicious smell of frying bacon from the catering-van carried on the crisp morning air. For, while it has been already stated that there was always *sufficient* food in the forest for the ever-hungry wolves – it should also be made plain that there was never, ever, too *much*.

It was then, at that very moment, as the wolf-pack lingered inquisitively in the fringe of pine trees close by the curious man-camp, sniffing greedily at the scent of sizzling bacon, that they spotted the largest, juiciest prospective meal that they had ever set hungry eyes upon. They had no idea what curious kind of animal it was that had presented itself before them, lying helpless on its back under the glare of arc-lamps in the clearing, feebly waving four huge pink-red claws in the air. They were aware only that it came under the general heading of food. Animal reasoning also assured them that they had as much right to the succulent meal as the several humans that stood round gazing down at it. The wolves decided therefore, then and there, to make their bid for what they considered to be theirs. Together as always, the pack bounded forward towards the clearing.

11

Strange to tell, as Harvey Miskin lay on the snow, floundering helplessly on his back, blinking owlishly behind his glasses inside his lobster head, he would have agreed, quite happily, to providing himself as a meal for the wolves. Why not? After all, he had already prayed for the ground to open and swallow him up. Why not indeed? There was little to choose, it seemed to him in those awful moments, between being eaten by a pack of wolves or swallowed down whole by Mother Earth.

Only a minute or so earlier, when he had left the make-up tent, he had been delighted to see Sharon Dexter, the girl that filled his dreams, standing over by the counter of the catering-van and munching on a bacon-roll. Deciding to join the actress for a quick snack before the first day's filming began, Harvey had set out towards her, walking unsteadily across the snow on his lobster-claw clad feet.

The actor had taken no more than five, or possibly six, unsure steps across the slippery, uneven ground, when awful tragedy had struck. He had lost his balance. His lobster-claw shod left foot, on encountering a little icy patch, had gone suddenly out of control. He had watched helplessly, through a slit in his plastic lobster head, as that same left foot had shot up in front of him – followed closely by the lobster claw that covered his right foot. Although it must all have been over in much less than a second, it had seemed to Harvey as if it had happened in slow motion – as if his body had hung horizontal, suspended in mid-air, before crashing to the ground.

Once on his back, Harvey Miskin had found himself lying helpless, like some unfortunate eight-foot pink-red beetle, unable to right himself. But what was worse about his humiliating situation – much, much worse – was that Sharon Dexter, instead of rushing forward to help him, had thrown back her head and laughed. And the more that the unhappy actor attempted to roll himself over onto his lobster-pink front, the more the actress was convulsed with laughter.

Harvey Miskin had never been so abjectly embarrassed in the whole of his life.

"Lie still!" called Hiram P. Hurtzburger, from the tent flap of his production office. "Don't move! You'll damage the costume!"

Taking their cue from Sharon, property-men began to laugh with her; camera-crewmen held their sides and guffawed. Hearing the noise, make-up girls and wardrobe mistresses appeared from out of their huts and tents and were also vastly entertained.

It was at that moment, while feebly pawing with his claws at the air, that Harvey Miskin had prayed that the ground might open and mercifully swallow him. It was less than a split-second later that he had glimpsed through the peep-hole in his lobster head,

the pack of wolves bounding out from the shelter of the pine trees and towards the floodlit clearing. It seemed, to the actor, almost as if his prayer was about to be answered.

Had it not been for the joint intervention of Count Alucard and Kitty Beaumont, Harvey Miskin might well have fallen prey to the wolf-pack. For it was none other than the vegetarian vampire Count himself who, having seen what was about to happen from the vantage point of his tree-stump, ran to the fallen actor's assistance. At the same time, Kitty, who had also had an excellent view of what had happened from behind the catering-van's counter, acted on impulse. Snatching up as many of the previously prepared bacon-rolls as she could hold, she threw them, one by one, into the path of the advancing wolves.

Whether it was Count Alucard's action in rushing to the actor's assistance that dissuaded the wolves from biting into the plastic shell; or whether it was the waitress's quick thinking that saved the day, shall never be known. Most probably, it was a mixture of the two.

What can be stated, is that at the very moment that the wolves paused to snap and snarl and snatch at the bacon-rolls – and at the same time as the Count assisted the grateful Harvey Miskin to his feet – other diversions began to take place all at once. For it was in those same hectic moments that the angry villagers arrived on the scene, with their scythes, pitchforks and other makeshift weapons, shouting for Count Alucard's blood.

"Death to the vampire!" bellowed a weather-beaten shepherd, waving his crook above his head.

"Death to *all* vampires!" croaked the village's oldest inhabitant, punching the air with his walking-stick.

"C'mon, Brad!" cried Sheriff Tucker, rising to his feet as the villagers poured into the clearing, obscuring the sheriff's view of the Count. "Let's you and me go get him!"

"I blame you for all of this!" growled Henri Rumboll at Alphonse Kropotel as they, too, lumbered to their feet and stumbled through the snow to join the throng.

"Me! What have I done?" mumbled the unhappy police sergeant. "Why should I be blamed because my wife cannot hold her tongue?"

There was an end to talking then as pandemonium took over. In their haste to get at Count Alucard, villagers stepped on wolves' paws while, in their eagerness to snap up morsels of bacon-roll, wolves snapped at villagers' heels. The film people, in their efforts to prevent the villagers knocking over their cameras and arc-lamps, succeeded only in stepping back themselves and knocking over not only arc-lamps and cameras but also all the other technical equipment necessary to the making of a film. Tents were trampled down. Huts collapsed under the weight of pressing bodies. Sheriff Tucker and Deputy Crick, having discovered that they were not alone in their desire to apprehend the vampire Count, strove hard to push back Sergeant Kropotel and Mayor Rumboll who, in their turn, attempted to force themselves past Tucker and Crick.

Somewhere close to the very centre of the turmoil

in the clearing, Count Alucard found time to remember his manners as he greeted Kitty who had managed to force her way towards him.

"Dear lady, what a pleasant surprise," began the Count, still keeping a steadying hand on Harvey Miskin who was struggling to stand upright on his lobster claws. "How delightful it is to see you again – despite these rather aggravating circumstances."

"Thanks for helping me out too," said Harvey Miskin to the waitress, his voice muffled behind his lobster head, "I mean with the bacon-rolls and the wolves."

"That's okay," replied Kitty with a smile and a shrug. "I just felt that *somebody* needed to do something – what with all of those folk standing laughing at you an' all."

The actor, remembering that it had been Sharon who had laughed the loudest and longest at his predicament, nodded slowly and blinked back a tear which, happily, went unnoticed behind his lobster mask.

"All things considered, dear lady," said Count Alucard, with a little bow, "I think it might be wise for us to speedily take our leave of these proceedings – unless you yourself have reasons for wishing to remain?"

"No *way*!" replied the waitress, glancing around at the heaving mass of men and women and wolves. "But how *do* we get away from here?"

"Take my hand, dear lady," said the Count. "And allow me to provide the vehicle that will assist us in our escape."

"Would that happen to have an extra seat?" asked

Harvey Miskin from inside his lobster head. "I don't think that there's much to detain me here any longer either."

Count Alucard smiled and nodded then, holding Kitty Beaumont's hand in one of his, and supporting Harvey Miskin with his other, the Count led the way through the pushing, shoving throng of animals and humankind.

The last thing that Harvey Miskin caught sight of through the narrow slit in his lobster mask, was the figure of Sharon Dexter somewhere in the thick of the mass of bodies, holding both hands protectively up to her head and yelling: "My hair! My hair! Don't anybody mess up my hair – I spent two hours in make-up this morning!"

Minutes later, had any one of the still struggling figures in the clearing chanced to look down at the lower stopes of the mountain, then he or she would have seen a coffin-lid makeshift sledge with three passengers on board: a black-cloaked man, a pretty girl and a giant-sized pink-red lobster – skimming over the smooth snow towards the village and to safety.

"I don't see how we're ever going to continue with the movie, Mr Hurtzburger," sighed Howard Frost, some time later, when peace and tranquillity had returned to the clearing.

All around them lay the damaged equipment; the upturned cameras, the trampled-down tents, the over-turned huts – all of which gave evidence of the rumpus that had taken place. The villagers and the wolves had long since gone their separate ways.

Sheriff Tucker and Deputy Crick had packed their things into the hire-car and set off along the mountain road on the start of their long journey home. Sergeant Kropotel and Mayor Rumboll had also given up all hope of laying hands on the vampire and had trudged down the mountain slopes towards the village.

"Transylvania ain't no good place to make a movie anyhow," growled the famous film producer, feeling inside his overcoat pocket for a fresh cigar and discovering, to his annoyance, that his entire stock had been crushed in the melée.

"If you aren't going to make the vampire picture, Hiram, does that mean that I won't get another fur coat?" asked Hetty Hurtzburger who, having earlier spotted the wolf-pack eyeing her oddly, had spent most of that morning uncomfortably perched halfway up a pine tree.

"Nuts to fur coats," snapped Hiram P. Hurtz-burger. "From here on in, Hetty – fur coats are *out*. We're broke!"

"My dear, dear lady!" enthused Count Alucard to old Mrs Prendergast as he took in the familiar sur-roundings. "It's exactly as I left it – nothing has changed!"

It was true. The cosy cottage bedroom was *exactly* as it had been on the day that he had fled from it, almost a year before. The old-fashioned, enormous walnut wardrobe with its matching chest of drawers on top of which there stood, on a crocheted doily, a small chipped vase containing a selection of wild-flowers. The same framed picture of two kittens peeping out of a basket, hanging over the brass bedstead, and the pretty patchwork quilt spread neatly over the made-up bed. Best of all, perhaps, there was the old, familiar scent of honeysuckle drifting in through the open window.

"I've tried to keep everything as it was," said the old lady with a smile. "I've always hoped that I might see you back again one day."

"I'm so glad to be here," said the Count, softly.

"East, West – home's best."

"Except, of course," began the Count, a trifle sadly, "this isn't really my home."

"Home is where the heart is."

"Do you know something, dear lady?" said Count Alucard, brightening. "I do believe that's true."

"I blame you for all of this," grumbled Mayor Rum-boll, looking across the empty village square. The snow had long since gone but the tourists had not returned to Rumptoft.

"Me!" replied Sergeant Kropotel, hurt and astonished. "Why blame me?"

"Because if it had not been for your interference, and that film had been made, Rumptoft might have received some publicity – that would have brought the tourists flocking back to Rumptoft."

"That wasn't my fault! That was all because of my wife."

"Don't blame me!" snapped Irma Kropotel, appearing at her husband's elbow as she shepherded their two children out into the square. "You were the one who started all that nonsense about the vampire threatening the lives of these poor chicks. I ask you? Do they *look* as if their lives are threatened?"

"May we go up and play on the mountainside this afternoon, mother?" asked Konrad.

"Oh, mother – may we – *please*?" added Gretel.

"Of course you may, my lambkins," replied Mrs Kropotel, all of her chins a-wobble as she flashed her husband a challenging look, daring him to argue with her. But the police sergeant knew when it was wise to hold his tongue. "Go up there whenever you wish," she added.

Konrad and Gretel ran off, hand in hand, towards the narrow road that led up towards the mountain slopes. They had been up to the castle ruins many times that summer, but they had never again encountered the curious, kindly gentleman with whom they had shared one wintry afternoon.

But that did not matter to them. There was birdsong in the trees and there were rabbits in abundance in the undergrowth. The children splashed in the mountain streams and frolicked under the sun. They were glad that they were young.

"Could I have another cup of coffee?" ventured Sheriff Wayne Tucker, pushing his empty cup across the counter of the roadside diner.

"I surely would appreciate another cup of coffee too," added Deputy Sheriff Bradford Crick.

"Coffee's finished," snapped Doris, the new waitress at the diner. "And *I* would appreciate it if you two would get off about your duties and allow me to get this place cleaned up."

Sheriff Tucker sighed as he eased himself off the red plastic-covered tall stool at the counter. Deputy Crick did the same. The two Kansas lawmen moved off together, through the diner's door and out towards the police car which was parked outside.

Life was back to normal for the two American policemen. There were bank robbers to be apprehended and car thieves to be pursued along the motorways. All the same, it sometimes seemed to them as if something was missing from their lives – like an empty coffee-cup being refilled with a friendly smile.

"I say! That *is* good news," said Count Alucard as he scanned the contents of the airmail letter which the new and cheerful postman had delivered to him that morning.

"What's that, Mr Alucard?" asked old Mrs Prendergast, setting down the tray of homemade

180

lemonade and coconut macaroons on the rustic garden table. Her paying guest had settled himself in a deckchair in order to catch up on the stack of back-numbers of *The Coffin-Maker's Journal* which had piled up during his absence and which she had carefully set aside, awaiting his return.

"You may remember," continued the Count, "my telling you about two friends I made during my travels: Kitty Beaumont and Harvey Miskin?"

"Why, yes, I believe I do," replied the old lady as she sat down in the basket chair which the Count had thoughtfully carried out from the cottage. "Miss Beaumont was the waitress, wasn't she? And Mr Miskin was the nice young gentleman who was going to portray the part of the lobster in the film in which you yourself almost starred?"

"That is correct, dear lady," replied the Count, leaning forward to pour out lemonade into the two waiting tumblers. "Well then – it would appear that the two of them have gone into business together. They have opened a seafood restaurant, called The Lobster-Pot, on the Bay of San Francisco."

"How nice!" said old Mrs Prendergast. "I do hope that it's successful for them."

"But that is only half the story – it seems that they are also getting married."

"I'm sure, from all that you have told me about them both, that they will make each other very happy."

"All's well that end's well," said the Count, munching on a coconut macaroon. "I am only pleased that it was I who was instrumental in bringing the

181

two of them together – at least it makes it seem as if *some* good has come out of my journeying around the world."

"I have been thinking about all that too," said the old lady then, after pausing to sip at her lemonade, she continued: "And about your wishing that people could get to know you as the sort of kind and gentle and considerate person that I know you to be."

"You flatter me, dear lady," said the Count, with a wistful smile. "But pray continue."

"Well then – how would it be if you were to put down all of your adventures in a book? Exactly as you told them to me? After all, I found them to be extremely interesting and exciting. And folk would then be able to judge for themselves what kind of a person you really are."

"Write a book?" Count Alucard frowned. "I am not entirely certain that I have the capacity for such a venture."

"You wouldn't have to *write* the book yourself," said the old lady. "You could tell your story to a proper author and he would set it down for you. I've even thought of a title."

"And what might that be?" asked the Count with a smile. Really! His landlady seemed so keen on the venture that he hardly cared to disappoint her.

"*The Vampire's Revenge*."

"*The Vampire's Revenge?*" Count Alucard frowned as he nibbled, thoughtfully, on a second coconut macaroon. "I am not entirely sure that 'revenge' is quite the right word," he continued at last. "After all, I am not myself a vengeful person

182

– the events that happened on my travels were not wrought by my hand but seemed to happen of their own accord. You don't suppose, do you, dear lady, that *The Vampire That Would Not Harm So Much As A Fly* might be a more apt and fitting title?"

"Oh no, Count Alucard, most definitely not," replied the white-haired, apple-cheeked old lady with a firm shake of her head. "I have a sister who works behind the counter of a public library in Shrewsbury. I am sure that she would tell you that a short and snappy title is one that is much more sought after by borrowers than a title that is long and cumbersome."

"*The Vampire's Revenge*," Count Alucard repeated the title over to himself. "It does have a certain ring to it."

"And you do want as many people as possible to know the truth about you, don't you?"

"Indeed I do, dear lady," replied the vegetarian vampire Count. "I desire that most of all in the entire world."

"I have to go indoors," said old Mrs Prendergast. "I'm preparing a Summer Pudding for lunch. I thought that you might care for some cold custard to go with it?"

"Mmmmmm! Wouldn't I just!"

"Well then, why don't you just sit out here and give some thought to what I've said?"

Count Alucard agreed to do just that. He promised the kind-hearted old lady that he would think long and hard about the possibility of his speaking to someone regarding the publication of a book which

183

would contain all of his recent adventures. He also gave her his solemn word that he would give some thought too, to the title of that book.

But there was no immediate hurry. It was, after all, the pleasantest and most enjoyable of summer mornings. The sun was hanging overhead, blazing down from out of a cloudless sky. There was no sound to be heard – apart from the occasional drone of a bumblebee as it drifted, on the gentlest of summer breezes, above the blaze of colour in the cottage-garden flower beds.

Count Alucard let out a little sigh of self-satisfaction as he settled himself, comfortably, in his deck-chair. The decision about the book and its choice of title could come later. But first things first. If he was going to stay at dear Mrs Prendergast's for any length of time, he would need to order himself a brand-new coffin.

Stretching out a pale, slim hand, he picked up the top copy from the pile of back-numbers of *The Coffin-Maker's Journal* and began, idly, to flick through the illustrated pages . . .

Other great reads ⟵ *from* **Red Fox**

Further Red Fox titles that you might enjoy reading are listed on the following pages. They are available in bookshops or they can be ordered directly from us.

If you would like to order books, please send this form and the money due to:

ARROW BOOKS, BOOKSERVICE BY POST, PO BOX 29, DOUGLAS, ISLE OF MAN, BRITISH ISLES. Please enclose a cheque or postal order made out to Arrow Books Ltd for the amount due, plus 75p per book for postage and packing to a maximum of £7.50, both for orders within the UK. For customers outside the UK, please allow £1.00 per book.

NAME_____

ADDRESS_____

_____

Please print clearly.

Whilst every effort is made to keep prices low, it is sometimes necessary to increase cover prices at short notice. If you are ordering books by post, to save delay it is advisable to phone to confirm the correct price. The number to ring is THE SALES DEPARTMENT 071 (if outside London) 973 9700.

Other great reads *from* **Red Fox**

Have a chuckle with Red Fox Fiction!

FLOSSIE TEACAKE'S FUR COAT   Hunter Davies

Flossie just wants to be grown-up, like her big sister Bella – and when she tries on the mysterious fur coat she finds in Bella's bedroom, her wildest dreams come true . . .
ISBN 0 09 996710 3   £2.99

SNOTTY BUMSTEAD   Hunter Davies

Snotty's mum has gone away leaving him with lots of cash and the house to himself! Burgers for breakfast, football in the front room – and no homework! But can he keep the nosey grown-ups away?
ISBN 0 09 997710 9   £2.99

HENRY HOLLINS AND THE DINOSAUR
Willis Hall

Little did Henry think, when he found the fossilized egg at the seaside, that it was actually a fossilized DINOSAUR egg! He had even less idea that it would be no time at all before he would be travelling up the moorway on a dinosaur's back!
ISBN 0 09 911611 1   £2.99

THE LAST VAMPIRE   Willis Hall

The Hollins family are on holiday in Europe, and all goes well until they stay the night in a spooky castle, miles from nowhere. Even worse, they discover that they are in the castle belonging to Count Alucard.
ISBN 0 09 911541 7   £2.99

TRIV IN PURSUIT   Michael Coleman

One by one, the teachers at St Ethelred's School are vanishing, leaving cryptic notes behind. "Triv" Trevellyan smells something fishy going on and is determined to find out just what is happening!
ISBN 0 09 991660 6   £2.99